A HOT PROPERTY

Judy Feiffer

A HOT PROPERTY

Random House New York

Library of Congress Cataloging in Publication Data
Feiffer, Judy. A hot property.   I. Title.
PZ4.F29735Ho   [PS3556.E419]   813'.5'4   72–10930
ISBN 0–394–48376–6

To Bob Loomis

A HOT
PROPERTY

ESTHER OPPENHEIM
read *Bonjour Tristesse* when
she was fourteen. She turned off the light and held the
book close to her small bud breasts. She thought of
Françoise Sagan bolting the hallowed halls of the Sor-
bonne and taking a racing dive into life. But Sagan
had been older, perhaps eighteen, while Esther had
not even started to menstruate. She thought a lot
about Sagan. She'd read somewhere that Françoise
had spent one drowsy summer reading *Remembrance*

of Things Past and that this had given her the impetus to write. Esther decided to pass her own time until maturity's arrival by reading Proust. She bought *Swann's Way*, but by the time the narrator was gorging himself on the last crumbs of his *madeleine*, Esther had lost interest. She tried again. She yawned her way through his lunches with his grandmother in Combray; She joined him on his endless walks along the Guermantes Way; achieved with him his first awesome look at the Duchesse de Guermantes; and then, on page one hundred and thirty-five, nature struck! On page one hundred and thirty-five of *Swann's Way*, Esther became a woman. She hastily abandoned *Remembrance of Things Past* and began to make plans for her own anticipated plunge into life.

What she needed was an introduction. A generous soul to unlock the doors of experience. The simplest place to start was her father's client list. Its wealth, erudition and achievement dazzled her. She reviewed its names, wondering who would prove the active spirit in the service of her cause.

Faces and credits flashed before her: a Nobel Peace Prize winner, two Pulitzer authors, seven National Book Award nominees (one winner), four screenwriters, but only two Oscars. Broadway playwrights published by Random House with off-Broadway breaking through the ranks. The list was heavy on memoirs: a four-star general (Vietnam), a double agent (World War II), countless consciences of America up from the counterculture and leaping onto the

Sunday *Times* best-seller list. Poets, politicians and pornographers (soft-core). Faces and credits flashed by Esther like the worn cards in a nickel peepshow. Each card a milestone in her father's prestigious career. The famous array parading by gladdened her little heart with joy. Her pulse quickened at the infinite possibilities.

GORDON OPPENHEIM was up at seven-thirty. He put on his jockstrap, sweat socks, his Puma jogging shoes, and a light cotton shirt and shorts. His tall, fit body had barely changed since his graduate years at Princeton. The man was in his prime.

He glanced at Faye lying under the Porthault coverlet. She was sleeping, or pretending.

"Faye," he said cautiously.

She opened an eye and looked at her husband as

if he were an isometric triangle, a leftover from high
school algebra.

"How about a jog around the reservoir?"

Faye burped.

"Charming." Gordon regarded his wife with
weary, residual eyes. She was something that had
whammed him a long time ago.

She felt his cold eye on her. She felt him looking
at her as if she were an expired contract, searching
out a clause for future option in small print.

"Come with me," he said. "We'll jog together.
It'll pull you into shape."

"You're crazy," she said.

"I may be crazy, but I don't like to be seen with
Marie Dressler at openings."

Faye raised herself and looked in the mirror. In
the morning she ran loose—hair, belly, small pockets
of flesh that drop during the night. But she could pull
it together for that old look. She could still walk into
a room and have every eye on her.

"Male menopause," she said. "That's what's both-
ering you."

Suddenly he was beside her, the friendly country
doctor. He was tender, concerned. He took her hand.
(Bedside manner, brilliant.) "I pulled you out of Hol-
lywood fifteen years ago and you turned into a potato.
But you got yourself together and you wrote *The
Big Bed*. You can do it again."

"What again?"

"Write."

"I'm not a writer."

"You were once."

"Never."

"All you need is an idea." (He stroked the dying patient.)

"I'm not a writer. I wrote one book but that doesn't make me a writer. I don't know the first thing about it. What are you trying to do to me, Gordon?"

"Look, Faye. I'm going to the Coast next week. The house'll be quiet. I want you to work off some of your goddamn boredom then."

"I have nothing to say. I've always had nothing to say. I always will have NO-THING-TO-SAY! You must be insane!"

"You know why I fell in love with you? Because you'd been beaten up. You'd been lived in." He was relentless, stroking her hand, his voice inspiring. He was willing her back into life. *"The Restless Wife.* There's your title. The intelligent wife—too old for women's lib, but conscious of the waste, the emptiness, the deadening routine of her upper-class existence. Faye, the studios are screaming for middle-aged women properties. I'll buy you a mink with the advance."

Faye looked at her husband, cold light bursting through the blind panic. He really was one hell of an agent. She felt a moment of neutral affection and remembered why she'd married him.

Like a flashback, some of the old lovers passed in front of her. They looked like a bread line during the

Depression. And suddenly there was Gordon. He'd appeared like a Saint Bernard with a bottle of brandy around his neck and a tin of Band-Aids in his paw. He licked her wounds and carried her off, away from cheap hotels and old roadsters to a king-size bed in a duplex penthouse. Exhausted from the wear and tear of not making it in Babylon, she simply collapsed into the good life with Gordon Oppenheim.

"Faye, *you can do it again*. There *are* some second acts in American lives." (F. Scott Fitzgerald, the homely philosopher.)

She believed him for a moment. She thought she could do it. He kissed her gently (he was into artificial resuscitation) and then ran off to the reservoir for his three-mile, two-lap daily constitutional.

ESTHER scanned her father's library. Its famous names were like family. Familiar as her mother, consigned to her room, her bed, her gadgets and magazines, accoutrements of a life spent in limbo. Familiar as her father's shadowy nighttime appearance.

Its authors had nervously paced the burnished floors, dropped Havana ash on the deep pile carpet, leaked Jack Daniel's on the chamois couch. They had drunk, eaten, peed, complained and wept. Fame had been a chronic guest.

Paul Samuels, a blue workshirt among the tuxedo fronts, aroused her. She didn't know why. He wasn't a wit spectacled in heavy tortoise shell, he wasn't this year's hot property. All he had was a Pulitzer Prize in nonfiction dating back to 1944. And he looked like George C. Scott, beaten, tough and far away. Esther read the flap copy on his books. He'd been everywhere: Battle of the Bulge, with Stilwell in China, Algeria, Africa, Israel, Poland, Ethiopia, France. He'd been there.

After the war he'd turned to fiction which, alas, never caught fire. No one discussed his books. The *Times* buried him on page thirty-two. He was a war ace. They couldn't forget it.

He lived modestly on Riverside Drive with a restless wife. She liked to move but she moved alone, for Paul felt burnt out, and he stayed on the Drive with the gusting winds that beat across the Hudson into his room.

Esther found his number in her mother's address book. "Mr. Samuels, this is Esther Oppenheim."

"Hello, Esther," he said. "I'm glad you called."

"Why?"

"Laura's away. I'm lonely."

"Loneliness can be depressing," she said.

"Writing's depressing," he said. "Come on over and cheer me up. Grab a cab. I'll pay you back when you get here."

Nursing a lonely and depressed writer. What a

break! "Okay," she said. "But forget the cab fare. I have money."

The cab let her out at Riverside and Eighty-fourth. She passed a dozing doorman and took the elevator to fourteen. The front door was ajar. She entered, closing it behind her, and passed empty, rambling rooms until she saw him. Stale newspapers, bulging wastebaskets, empty beer cans, withered orange peels and smashed cigarette butts surrounded him. He was reading. Esther sat beside him.

"I've been feeling lousy," he said.

"I came to nurse you."

"I need it."

"Doesn't your wife do it?"

"She used to. Now I nurse her."

"Is she sick?"

"Bored."

Esther marveled at the idea of being bored with Paul Samuels. A man so weathered and used. A man who'd thrown his body into the bloody waters of Normandy, recorded the horrors at Dunkirk. She shivered at the thought of his endurance and his pain.

"What are you reading?" she asked shyly.

"*The Story of O*," he said.

"What's that?"

"Not for kids."

"I just look like a kid."

"Okay," he said. He turned to page one and gave her the book.

She skimmed it.

Her lover one day takes O for a walk in a section of the city where they never go—the Montsouris Park. . . . they notice . . . a car which . . . resembles a taxi.

"Get in," he says.

She gets in. . . . The taxi moves off slowly, the man still not having said a word to the driver. But he pulls down the shades of the windows on both sides . . . and the shade on the back window. . . .

"You also have on too many clothes. Unfasten your stockings and roll them down to above your knees. Here are some garters."

By now the taxi has picked up speed, and she has some trouble managing it. . . . Finally, though, the stockings are rolled down, and she's embarrassed to feel her legs naked and free beneath her silk slip. . . .

"Unfasten your garter belt," he says, "and take off your panties."

Esther looked at Paul.

"Go on," he said. "It gets better."

. . . "You shouldn't sit on your slip and skirt. Pull them up behind you and sit directly on the seat."

The seat is made of some sort of imitation leather which is slippery and cold: it's quite an extraordinary sensation to feel it sticking to your thighs. Then he says:

"Now put your gloves back on."

. . . she doesn't dare ask why Rene just sits
there without moving or saying another word,
nor can she guess what all this means to him—
having her there motionless, silent, so stripped
and exposed, so thoroughly gloved, in a black car
going God knows where. . . .

"Good stripped prose," Paul said, taking *O* away
from her.

The leather seat stuck in her mind. She wanted
to read more.

"Take it," he said unexpectedly. "It's a present."

"Thanks." She avoided his look.

"Are you afraid of me?"

"You're different."

He laughed. "Ebbing writers have always ap-
pealed to romantic young girls."

"I've read your books," she lied. "You were a
hero."

"You like that, don't you?"

"Do you mean do I like you?"

He took her hand. He pushed it toward his crotch.
She didn't resist.

"Do you know what heroes like?"

"Battle and victory."

"Scared?"

"Sure," she said. "Wouldn't you be?" Her eyes
were glowing. She thought of the girl in the taxi, the
cold, slippery leather against her thigh.

"You want to know, don't you? You want to feel

it, an invasion. You want to hear the shells, see the volleys, smell the violence and mutilation."

She didn't answer. She kept thinking of the girl in the taxi, stripped and exposed and going God knows where.

Her hand lay on his penis but now it was hard as a bullet. He pulled down her Fruit of the Loom underpants and turned her over. He burst into her like a grenade and she screamed in panic and pain.

ON MONDAY a limousine pulled up at eight to drive Gordon to Kennedy Airport. Esther disappeared minutes later. The housekeeper had not arrived. Faye made herself coffee, went into Gordon's den and sat in front of the eighteenth-century Queen Anne elm desk. She lit a cigarette and cast an eye on crisp dust jackets that covered the walls. They represented many of Gordon's clients.

One, *The Big Bed*, was Faye's. It had been ignored in hardback but the reprint rights sold for thirty-five thousand dollars. It had been published in four languages with an enormous sale in Japan. And it had been sold to the movies.

She sat in a trancelike state for about an hour, occasionally looking out the window at the nurses and baby carriages. Disconsolate, she went into the kitchen for another cup of coffee. Back in the den, she looked at the typewriter, Italian portable, looked out the window as the park filled with bird watchers, joggers and drunks. They looked like incidental specks. She avoided looking at the shiny, dusted books, and finally, desperately, went back to bed and pulled the covers over her head. Christ, only Monday. She felt depression crawl into bed with her. She felt it nuzzle her, fondle her and dig a path into her stomach. It pressed close, closer, and before it scored its mark, she fled back into the library and sat once more at the polished elm desk. The drunks were sprawled across the benches, the nurses had taken their carriages and moved on, the joggers were deep into sprint and Faye said "Shit" and went into the bathroom. She showered and dressed and pushed the elevator button as if it read PANIC. She walked among dog lovers, lovers clutching, love spilling over onto paths and fields, and she sank back into time, time before Gordon, before she'd been bibbed and tucked into her sable nest.

Sunlight zigzagged along her way, sudden bright patches, but Faye felt no bright moments. As she wandered back through the years, she found it difficult to distinguish one face from another. The pain of those times had dulled over like scar tissue, and what remained was blurred. It was as if she had anesthetized those youthful years, banishing memory, leaving a stainless and stateless past.

She'd been cocooned up in her duplex castle in creamy velvets and satin sheets for fifteen years; the hostess in Gordon's house, entertaining Gordon's guests and clients. They were his golden oil rigs plowing into fertile earth and extracting the rich oil which Gordon refined into dollars and cents. Each book sold to the movies, each play opening to a million-dollar benefit advance, each historical novel astride the best-seller lists, ten percent of all that belonged to Gordon. Gordon was royalty among agents, and his writers worked industriously, weaving golden yarn for him to take to the market and sell for the highest price. And on every sale, right off the top, like fresh cream, Gordon scooped ten percent. Faye, beautiful and in decline, loved the money, but spent restless, nervous days warding off sudden nauseous seizures.

Dispirited, she changed directions and walked toward Broadway. She walked along the nervous, dirty street and stopped to look into the windows of Zabar's. She passed the dangling salamis and directed her attention to the selection of condiments, imported spices from Malaysia and Pakistan, pickled sensations from Turkey and India. Spread before her was a range of global delicacies. It was like passing the ports of call on a tramp steamer. She chose spicy fig and walnut chutney and went home.

She went into her room, lay down and tried again, hoping to find a name or a face that could resurrect some feeling. Wasted and empty, she went to a movie.

TUESDAY Faye slept un-
til ten-thirty. She made her-
self coffee and toast, placed them on a tray and slipped
back into bed. Today she'd start afresh. She sipped
delicately at the espresso and lit a cigarette. She sank
back into the downy pillows, closed her eyes, reaching
for some incident, a lover, a house, a face. A screen
gauze protected her from those neighborhoods with
worn shingled houses.

Surely there'd been more to her life than those

tawdry, forgotten nights, loveless fucking for a small career. But as she tried going back, she saw no faces, remembered no bodies. The few years of hustling as a Hollywood starlet were followed by marriage to Gordon, and that was it, her little life, already partially recorded in her Hollywood opus. Discouraged, she dressed and scanned the *Times* movie section. *Seventh Heaven* was playing at the New Yorker. She dressed and walked briskly to Eighty-ninth Street. A sprinkling of kids and the geriatric crowd were there for the four o'clock show. The houselights dimmed and a soft and fuzzy image of the Fox logo appeared. Faye was suddenly very happy.

JANET GAYNOR

CHARLES FARRELL

in

SEVENTH HEAVEN

Directed by

FRANK BORZAGE

The soft, dimmed print was a silent film from the twenties. It was the story of Diane, beaten and bullied by her maniacal, drunken sister, rescued from near death by Chico, who had worked his way up from the sewers into the sunlit Paris streets. Chico, spirit of courage and upward mobility, takes the bedraggled waif to his garret, where he joyfully proclaims: "I work in the sewer but I live near the stars." On that line, Faye's first tear fell. It was followed by another. They felt warm as they rolled down her cheek. She felt her own heart beat.

Chico shows Diane how to balance herself on a catwalk that joins the Paris rooftops. "I never look down. Only look up. That's why I'm a very remarkable fellow."

Faye felt a quickening pulse. Her own existence drained away. The two figures on the screen slipped into her soul, possessed her, and she was reborn. She was one with Chico and Diane. United with them in a mythical kingdom. She was Diane, and Diane was Faye. Gordon no longer existed. There was only Faye and Diane and Chico. As Diane falls in love with Chico, Faye is Diane. Chico and Diane marry themselves under the stars, but it is Faye who is marrying Chico.

Chico says the simple marriage ritual: "Chico—Diane—Heaven."

Faye is falling apart. Tears are tumbling down, her heart is pounding furiously, a joyful tightening in her soul as she observes, participates in, the poignant marriage. Gordon is gone. Esther is gone. There is no tiara on the agent's wife now. The duplex penthouse is replaced by a Paris garret. There exists in that dark movie one body into which has flown the spirit of the screen, possessing it as a mythical spirit possesses the bodies of the damned.

Faye-Diane says to Chico: "I'm not used to being

happy. It's funny—it hurts." Pain pierces Faye. Movie pain, a joyful suffering that wrenches one's soul from daily endurance and plunges it into a world of glorious despair.

Tears fall on Faye's cheek. She shivers in heavenly pain. She is choked by love. Chico goes to war but Faye-Diane awaits him. Chico finally returns, and in a frenzy of romantic music, climbs the twisting staircase to his garret and his love. He is blind, but he is beautiful. The passionate theme of *Seventh Heaven* fills the theater and Faye sits in a pool of tears.

She sits in the worn velvet seat, her heart pounding savagely. She has been hypnotized into passion and love. She hums the music, hoping to preserve it as a perfect dream, and leaves the theater wiping back joyous and satisfying tears.

WHILE Faye was aching in *Seventh Heaven*, Esther was summoned from class to take a call from a Mr. Samuels.

"I haven't heard from you," he said.

"You didn't call."

"Come on over later. I miss you."

She hesitated. "I guess so. I don't know."

"We can play war games." He hung up.

❋   ❋   ❋

Esther found his front door locked. She rang the bell. Laura Samuels opened it.

What the hell is this?

Laura kissed Esther on the cheek and took her into the living room. "Paul's dressing. He'll be ready in a minute."

Esther wondered if they'd been making love. "How was your trip?"

"Beautiful. But a week in Rome is tiresome, provincial; all the interesting Romans are homosexual. There's hardly a hetero one can talk to. Very sad."

She's trying to tell me something. "You must have missed Paul."

Laura smiled. "Paul told me about your new friendship. I'm glad he found such a pretty friend. Otherwise he's so moody. I hate coming home to a cranky husband."

What had Paul said? Esther wondered.

Paul sauntered in, buttoning his shirt. "If it's not the agent's daughter! I see you girls have talked."

He poured himself a drink, sat down, his legs sprawled every which way. "I put in a good day. I'm bushed. How about a drink, Esther? Laura, get her a drink."

"Are you thirsty?" Laura asked.

"No, thank you."

"It'll relax you," Paul said.

"I'm relaxed."

"She's relaxed," Laura said. "Don't be a bore."

"I'm being hospitable."

"I don't want one, really."

They sat in silence. Esther looked at Laura, tall and slim, waves and curls tumbling down her neck; her breasts small and firm, her legs long and curved. She was as elegant as Paul was rough.

"I have a terrific yen," Paul said. "I've got a terrific yen to make a movie."

"Write a screenplay," Esther said suddenly. "You're a writer."

"I don't want to write a movie. I want to make one."

"You mean direct a movie?"

"Not exactly. That is, I've got a little story in mind, but I want someone else to direct it."

"Dad will get a director for it."

"It's not that sort of movie. I mean, a private thing. Something the Supreme Court wouldn't approve."

"The beavers on Eighth Avenue are cleaning up." She sounded like a staffer for *Variety*.

Paul smiled warmly at the agent's daughter. "I'm not talking beavers, Esther. I mean a personal film."

"I see," she said thoughtfully. "*You* want to be the star."

"Right. But I need a director."

"How about Laura?"

"She'll be my co-star."

"So you need a director."

"Right."

"Is there a script?"

". . . an idea. I'll tell the director what to do."

"And you want me to be the director."

"You're a talented girl, Esther. I thought it might be fun for you."

"I've never made a movie."

"You've worked an eight-millimeter camera, haven't you? That's all this is. Zoom in. Zoom out. Simple."

"Okay. But I want screen credit."

"Atta girl. Laura, get ready while I explain what I want."

Laura left the room and Paul took his camera from a cabinet. "Any moron can work this thing," he said. "All you do is push the button."

He handed it to her. She adjusted the viewfinder to her eye.

"Push the button," Paul said.

She pushed. There was a slight whirring sound.

"What I've got in mind is a cross between *The Story of O*—Know the book?"

She nodded, wondering if he'd forgotten or if he were playing games.

"—and *Belle de Jour*. See the movie?"

"I saw it with Mom. We both dug it."

"You're just the director I need. Now, when you think something is particularly interesting, you zoom in." He indicated a knob. "Turn this." She turned it. Paul loomed immense. "That's a close-up. Use it for detail. Now, when you concentrate on story, turn the knob in the other direction. That's a long shot. Now, props." He moved a custom-made leather chair into the middle of the room, opened his cabinet and took out a tangled branch.

"What's that?"

"Forsythia. Laura got them from the park. Look, there's a bud."

Esther examined the slender rods. A yellow nipple peeked from a ripening shoot. "Spring," she said.

"Yeah. Hey, Laura, we're waiting."

Laura came into the room. She was naked. Her long torso stretched from a thatch of curly black hair to breasts which hovered high like little stars.

What in hell! She looked at Paul. He smiled.

"Simple," Paul said. "An old-fashioned Hollywood plot: 'Boy meets girl, boy spanks girl, boy gets girl.' You can be as arty as you like, but remember: Story. Story. Story. Make sure you're not always in close-up."

He unzipped himself and stepped out of his pants, slid off his underwear and took off his shirt. He was limp. He stood next to Esther and began to re-instruct her.

Laura sat on the leather chair and beckoned to her husband. He kneeled between her legs and kissed her. She reached for his cock. She massaged it gently.

That rat! If he hadn't of fucked me, he wouldn't dare do this. Some hero!

"Shoot," Paul said.

Esther walked to the other end of the room and pressed the button.

"Too far," Paul said. "Don't get the whole room. Concentrate on us."

She walked several steps nearer.

"This isn't a David Lean production," Paul said. "Come close."

Esther did as she was told. Laura was fondling Paul's cock. He was kissing her. Esther pressed the button. The whirring distracted her. She felt envy. Paul stood, sizable and erect, and went for the forsythia. Esther followed him with the camera.

"On her," he yelled. "Keep it on her."

Esther focused on Laura, loose and elegant on the chair. Paul reentered the shot.

"Turn over," he said. Laura turned, spreading her buttocks upward. Paul grabbed them. He pressed his face against them. "Oh, God," he sighed. "Oh, Christ." Then he pulled away with the sad, pained look of an actor leaving his beloved for combat at the front, and firmly clasping the forsythia, hit her. "Long shot," he said. "This next bit in long shot."

As the rods hit Laura, she began to moan. She grabbed the top of the chair to support herself. There were welts on her behind. Esther hadn't remembered Paul that large. She felt damp. A feverish twitch, an ache. She remembered O sitting in the black car, silent, stripped, waiting for orders from her motionless lover.

Paul threw aside the forsythia and turned Laura over. He penetrated her and they swayed like tango dancers.

Esther moved into the groin area. The lovers moved in and out of frame. She fought to disengage herself, to abstract. She thought of Edward Weston's still lifes: his turnips, his parsnips. She concentrated on a loin, a buttock, Paul's cock as it emerged. Laura was sighing a woeful litany.

Suddenly the whirring stopped. Esther pushed the button but it was stuck. "It's jammed, something's jammed," she said happily.

"Shit," Paul said and extracted himself. He came to Esther and took the camera. He shook it and it started. Esther looked at Laura who seemed frozen in frame. Paul returned to her, still erect.

She shot from behind the chair, she straddled and stood above them, she knelt by their side.

Then the whirring stopped. "I'm sorry, Paul," she said. "It's jammed again."

"Shit!" Paul said. He exited, shook the camera, stabbed at it with his finger. "Goddamn Kodak," he said, but suddenly it started, so he handed it to Esther and plunged back into Laura. Energy renewed, all tenderness gone, there was a ferocity driving him into her body.

She was shooting tight into his genitals, and as she watched the two bodies she felt jealous and angry. Esther, she lectured herself, you are here for experience. Remember that. It's true that they're using me, but I'm using them too.

Paul's attack seemed endless. Then Laura grabbed him and seemed to push her insides into him. Paul poised for a final lunge and they both lay quiet.

"Damn," Esther said.

Paul got up. "What's the matter?"

"Nothing."

"Come here," Laura said.

"No."

"She's angry," Paul said. "Why in hell are you mad?"

"I'm not."

Laura came over to her. She placed her lips on Esther's. They were wet and warm. Laura's tongue slipped into her mouth like a pacifier. Esther felt like biting it in half.

"We won't make any more movies," Laura said. "Now and then Paul likes a little fun."

"I understand."

"You're not mad?"

She smiled a grim game little smile.

"Good," said Laura gently. She touched Esther's face. "Novels are so consuming. This relaxes him."

Paul was flopped onto the couch. His cock was limp and dangling over his thigh. "Come here," he said. "You did terrific. You don't have to be Kubrick on the first try."

"Writers are bastards," Esther said mockingly.

"You're learning," Paul said. "Tell your old man I'll have a first draft ready for him soon."

Paul blew her a kiss. But she'd already closed the door.

BROADWAY is harsh at twilight. Faye walked along the threatening street, holding on tightly to Chico and Diane. At Zabar's their image melted into the aroma of Nova Scotia salmon. She turned to the rack of condiments. As she browsed among the spices, Chico and Diane flew off to their garret in the sky and she was left amidst the jars of apricot and sour-cherry chutney.

"What a nice surprise," said an impish voice. Laura Samuels stood beside her. She picked a bottle of pickled mango and papaya off the shelf. "I'm told it compensates."

Faye readjusted her focus. She heard Laura say, "Why don't you and Gordon come over for a drink later?"

"Gordon's on the Coast."

"Come alone. Gordon's always talking business, anyway." Laura took her arm and pulled Faye along. There was a reckless energy in her stride. Faye tripped alongside like a leaf caught in the wind.

They walked to Eighty-fourth and Riverside and entered the building with twin turrets. The doorman was dozing. They took the elevator to fourteen and Laura opened the door. The place seemed empty.

"Yoo-hoo? I'm here." Laura went toward the kitchen.

Paul Samuels came down a long hall and said "Hi." It was inaudible.

He came toward Faye and placed an ordinary sort of kiss on her mouth. But as his body brushed against her, Faye felt a savage desire for him. She'd felt this way a long time ago. She didn't remember when. Paul seemed America. It poured from his brain like concrete, slid through muscle and nerve and came at her in a colossal grass-roots erection. He was politics and prairies, steel yards, cattle grazing. Paul was Mr. U.S.A. coming at Faye, poetic and hard. She pledged allegiance.

He pulled away and he knew that he had her. He took her hand and she thought he was going to press it against his joint. He thought so too. Instead he said, "Laura, where in hell are you? Faye's here."

He walked into the living room and Faye followed. She was irritated. She resented her fantasy, her surrender.

They sat silently and Laura came in with two drinks. She offered one to Faye and said, "Is Paul being moody? I can smell the silence down the hall."

"It's my double whammy," Paul said. "I'm giving Faye my double whammy."

"So long as it's not the clap," Laura said. "Paul sometimes gives that away too."

Paul looked at his wife as if he would like to give *her* a dose, a lethal one, but Laura nuzzled against him and said, "Laura's being bad." She arched her body against him like a cat, and Faye wanted to pull her away from Paul and throw her out the window.

"We share a taste for chutney," Laura said as she poured herself a drink. "We bumped tails at Zabar's."

"I just saw *Seventh Heaven*," Faye said. "It made me hungry."

"John Wayne makes me hungry," Paul said.

"You should write a Western," Faye said.

"Tell Faye about your little film," Laura said.

"You're a pain in the ass," he grumbled.

"Has Gordon seen it, your little film?" asked the agent's wife.

"*Mucho* dirty."

"Paul's a whiz at soft-core porno," Laura said.

"If he doesn't get a second Pulitzer he says he's turning to the hard stuff."

Faye ignored Laura. She looked at Paul with eyes promising Chico and Diane's HEAVEN. Laura caught the glow. She walked between them like a cloud.

"You must have had quite a few experiences of your own, Faye. *The Big Bed* was hardly an exercise in imagination."

Faye's promise of HEAVEN withered. She stood, starchly. Her tiara was back on its perch and the agent's wife said, "It was short and sweet. Maybe one day we can compare notes." She nodded to Laura.

Paul placed his hand on her shoulder and walked her to the door. As they stood waiting for the elevator he tried to rekindle America.

"Don't worry," Faye said. She gave him a look that was filled with bearskin rugs and a roaring fireplace, and then she stepped into the elevator as its doors opened to absorb her.

THE following morning, nine-ish, Faye picked up the phone on the first ring.

"When can I see you?" A mutter.

"Hello, Paul."

"Can you have lunch?"

"How about the Plaza?"

"The food stinks."

"I like the oysters."

"Okay. I'll be by in a cab. Wait downstairs."

Faye leaned back into the billowy pillows. She perched an Olivetti 22 on her lap. She inserted paper and started to type. Her fingers hit the keys with dexterity. She spent the morning jotting ideas, then replacing them. The keys burst the page like bullets. The paper filled with fantasy, with suppressed rage. Her low-grade depression was fighting for its life.

The agent's wife spent the morning preparing for battle. At twelve o'clock she slid from bed and collected her pages into a neat pile. She put the typewriter on her night table.

A fast shower, and an hour zealously changing contours: thinning cheekbones, expanding eyelids, smoothing fragrance into erogenous creases. She slipped into a wistful dress. It clung to her hips like a child's hug. Pleased, she hurried downstairs to meet Paul.

He was waiting in a cab. "I don't like the Plaza," he said.

"I like their oysters."

"You won't need oysters with me."

"I always need oysters."

He shut his eyes.

"Are you sick?" Faye asked. He nodded. "The oysters will help," she said. "They're Malpecques."

"Malpecques aren't in season. They won't help."

"You're depressed," Faye said. He nodded again. "Why are you depressed?" Paul was silent. "How can a Pulitzer Prize author be depressed?"

"You're making it worse."

"The act of creation should make you happy."

"I'm happy when I work. Then I wonder if it's good. Then I worry about the reviews. If I'm panned I worry how long it'll take me to recuperate from my depression. If I'm praised I worry that they'll get me on my next book. Then I worry if it'll be a best seller. Then I worry that no one will buy it for the movies. Finally, I'm desperate about what to write next."

"It must be hell being an artist," Faye said consolingly. She took his hand.

"It's torture."

The taxi pulled up to the Plaza and Paul paid the driver. They mounted the steps and twirled through the revolving doors.

"Oysters!" he said.

She smiled.

"Wait," he said. She stood under the blazing chandeliers as he went to the front desk to make arrangements for a room. The up elevator was slow. It was filled with blond girls and haggard men. "Four," Paul said and pushed her out. They walked down a long corridor toward Sixth Avenue. "I couldn't get a room with a view."

"Where's the bellboy?"

"We won't need one."

He unlocked 407 and they entered a beige room. It overlooked a shaft. Paul closed the curtains. He lunged onto the bed like a tired laborer and looked silently at Faye.

She walked toward him. "Where does your depression hurt?"

"All over."

She kissed him, pushing her tongue into his mouth.

"My depression still hurts."

"Where most?"

"Everywhere. It's a chronic depression."

She unzipped his fly and separated the split in his shorts. His prick flew out. "Do you keep him penned up all day?" she asked.

"If I don't, he'll bite the neighbors."

"Little wild beast." She slid her tongue over it like a confection. She sucked down to the core, fertilizing and probing the base as if she were preparing ground for seed.

"It's better," Paul moaned.

Her mouth stretched around his cock, massaged his circumcised fold, and then, like a magnetic suction, pulled him over the top. She swallowed the warm gissum as if it were a Malpecque oyster.

He rested in her as happy as if he'd hit number one on the Sunday *Times* best-seller list.

Faye lifted herself, but he pulled her back. He kissed her slowly, deeply, but she felt remote, as if she were in the wrong room.

"How's your depression?" she asked.

"It got raves. There's already an offer from Warner Brothers."

"All wild beasts need love," she said.

He unbuttoned his shirt and put her head on his sweaty chest. "Will you take off your clothes," he said gruffly.

"Later."

He sat up and pulled her dress over her head. She wore no brassiere. Her breasts were ripe, ready. But there was a time lag, the years had gently shaken them. Paul caressed each one and nipped at the furrowed tips. His little nips became shark sharp and Faye felt gummy and wet and she put her arms around him.

He was ready. She tucked a pillow under herself and he rose above her, leveled himself and penetrated. She was with him, moving with him, growing with his frenzy. He came strong and stronger and then she could go no more. She sobbed and then he sank on top of her, exhausted. He stayed there until his weight became painful. She pushed him and he pulled out and rolled over.

"That was good," he said. He looked at her. Her eyes were luminous. He guessed that she had come.

"It was like three days in Jamaica," she said, smiling a distant smile. America seemed one thousand miles away.

They were both quiet.

"Let's go, sweetie. I've got some work to do," he said.

Faye looked at his stocky body, firm, with a bit of soft around the waist. Grass Roots was going home, back to his typewriter. Grass Roots would get a good chapter out of this. Faye put on her wistful dress. She threw back her head. The tiara glowed.

"Hey," Paul said, "you look like an agent's wife."

He smiled at her. He'd gotten a good day's work in. She was terrific.

They went downstairs and he paid for the room.

She slipped into a satin dressing gown and hugged her Olivetti to her knees. She slipped another piece of paper into the machine.

She thought of Paul huddling over his typewriter, changing the color of her hair, the contours of her body, any significant detail. Paul was a professional. He'd write a story about them which Gordon might sell to *Playboy* for three thousand dollars. Paul could meet Faye next week and write another story. Enough meetings, a novel. What sweeter revenge on one's agent than to have an affair with his wife and make a potential fifty thousand dollars to boot. She thought about the money that Paul could make and she found her own suppressed energy.

"All right, Gordon, here I go!" She hurled herself into instant Lit; back into the bare beige room at the Plaza. She wondered how her body could find love while her soul felt so dead. Why couldn't he have been Tracy to her Hepburn, Bogart to her Bacall?

Gordon would get his book, damn it, no matter what the price.

Chapter I, she wrote. *How To Cheat on Your Husband and Stay Happily Married.*

WHEN Gordon came home that night he heard the faraway clicking of a typewriter. He went into his room and looked tenderly at Faye. He felt a beam of pleasure, like sunshine in December, at the sight of her in her satin robe, hitting the keys. She was finally at it. Publishers were panting for this new female sensibility.

His darling Faye looked at him coldly and said, "I'm working, Gordon." A warm glow flooded his balls.

He felt proud that this diamond in the rough, this Hollywood knockabout, was tamed. Mrs. Gordon Oppenheim, the agent's wife.

THE Harte was a private, coeducational school for over-achievers. The parents of the over-achievers were dazzling over-achievers themselves, and consequently the Parent-Teacher Association had for its membership the rich and famous or those making giant strides toward riches and fame. They poured hundreds of thousands of tax-exempt dollars into a scholarship fund, but every kid there smelled so rich and dressed so poor that it was hard to ferret out a real scholarship student.

Richard Karst, editor in chief of the school weekly, *Open Harte,* was the son of a Polish political exile, and the only student there who still believed in the American Dream. Esther passed him in the halls and felt his moral fervor come at her like a tropic heat. The more she saw of the serious editor, the more attractive she found him. She read his editorials paraphrasing ninteenth-century American visionaries and she fell in love.

Knowing he'd be riddled with integrity, she sent him an essay entitled "Sucking Your Way to Success." He rejected it with a contemptuous note.

She wrote him:

Dear Karst:

You rejected my essay, "Sucking Your Way to Success," but I have another idea. May I come and see you?

Sincerely,
Esther Oppenheim

A week passed before he answered.

Dear Miss Oppenheim:

I'm available for appointments at my office on Friday at 3:30.

Sincerely,
R. Karst

Esther entered the offices of the *Open Harte* and it seemed that the room was split in two. On one side giggling girls hovered over Zimmerman, the red-headed cartoonist, amidst the debris of scissors, glue and back issues of the *New York Times* and *Screw*.

The other side of the room was orderly and clean. At the farthermost corner sat Karst at his desk. Esther went to him.

"I'm Esther Oppenheim."

"I'm Karst. Sit down." She dragged over a chair. "What's your new idea?" he asked.

"I want to do a column called 'Bleeding Harte,' in which I give advice to the lovelorn, the lonely, the disenfranchised . . ."

"We are not a journal of mental health."

"How many masturbators still think it will fall off?" she asked. "How many girls fall asleep on fiery whipping fantasies?"

"You're an amusing person, Esther, but I run a serious paper."

"Serious? Are you serving an apprenticeship for the *Partisan Review*?"

He smiled at her sensibly. He looked like Leslie Howard. "I'm afraid it's a rotten idea, Esther. But keep trying."

She wrote down her telephone number on the sheet of copy he was correcting. "Your turn," she said and left the office.

She walked down the long hall to the street. Karst was a pedant. She saw his life stretching ahead of him. Harvard: editor of the Harvard *Crimson*. New York, and book reviews for the *Village Voice*. A piece for the Sunday *Times Magazine*. Articles for *Commentary*. A staff offer from *Harper's* or *Newsweek*. Marriage to a smart young editor at Random House. A seven-room apartment around Broadway and Eighty-sixth. A boy and a girl at Harte. A comfortable nest in the literary community. It was so neat, a West Side annuity. She felt a sudden childlike rage to take his life and wreak havoc.

FAYE OPPENHEIM answered the phone on Sunday.

"Esssther, for you."

Esther climbed out from under the *Times* drama section to take the call. "I wasn't sure you'd call, Karst. How about a movie? Okay. Pick me up at three o'clock."

At three, a Mr. Karst was announced through the intercom. Faye Cassidy Oppenheim opened the door.

Karst saw before him a candied, sensual presence. His virginity closed in on him like a jail. Esther's voice called them to come into the living room. Faye turned and Karst followed her like one moonstruck.

The large living room overlooked Central Park. Everything was soft and round and creamy. It felt like a velvet glove.

"What a pleasure," said Gordon Oppenheim.

The princely agent was a tall, stylish man. Karst felt small and skinny. Oppenheim's lavish dimples, melodic baritone and carefully groomed body reminded Karst of Henry Cabot Lodge.

"This is my father, Gordon Oppenheim. Daddy, this is Richard Karst. And you've already met Mother."

As he looked again at Faye, Karst felt internal amputation. He pulled his voice up from his wee wee where it had slid like an oyster. "We're going to the movies," he stuttered.

"Oh?" said Faye over an arched eyebrow. "What?"

"*A Star Is Born,* at the New Yorker."

"A family favorite. You'll like it," Gordon said, smiling. "That's a handsome tie. Try Battaglia for ties one day. I think you'll be surprised."

Karst felt like a refugee again. He looked at Gordon; his tailored ease and assurance made him seem as if he had swallowed America whole.

Esther sensed the chaos in her friend. It was a small triumph. She took his elbow and eased him into the hall.

A STAR IS BORN is my movie," she said.

"How can it be yours?"

"When I was born, Mother insisted I was to be named Esther after Esther Blodgett who's Janet Gaynor before she changes her name. Daddy said, 'Absolutely not!' I was to be called Vicky, after Vicky Lester who Janet Gaynor–Esther Blodgett changes her name to. Mother said she could never identify with a phony Hollywood name like Vicky Lester, she could only identify with Esther Blodgett. Daddy said Esther Blodgett was even more phony because it was Hollywood's condescending idea of what people in Middle America are called. They had a terrible fight. Mother said Daddy was a snob and that if he insisted on Vicky Lester, then she'd call me Rin Tin Tin. So he gave in, so here I am."

"They should have called you Esther Lester."

"Why, Karst! That'll be my nom de plume on my first screenplay."

"Your mother's really beautiful."

"I suppose so, in a sleazy sort of way."

"That's awful, Esther."

"I'm awful, Karst. It'll make me a good writer."

"You seem awfully sure about writers."

"Dad's in the business."

Karst was silent. He wanted to get back to Faye. "Was your mother an actress?"

"Faye Cassidy. You never heard of her. She was a sub-B movie star. Studios like Monogram and Republic, she worked for them. She wasn't in Hollywood for long, because she met Daddy and gave up acting to get married."

"Doesn't she miss being a star?"

"She was only a starlet. I suppose she missed it for a while but Daddy got her to write a book about Hollywood instead. She said it cured her."

"Can I read it?"

"Yeah. It's awful. *The Big Bed.* It's a *Grand Hotel* kind of idea, but instead of passing through a hotel

everybody passes through a bed. My father· sold it to
the movies and they changed the name to *The Big
Table,* and instead of a big bed all the characters sit
around a big table, or under it, in a famous Hollywood
nightclub. It wasn't any good. When I grow up I'm
going to have affairs with powerful men. I'll write
celebrated memoirs."

"I hope you have a liberal husband."

"Ha!" she laughed. "Each of my husbands will
be more famous than the last. With each famous husband, a notorious memoir. I can hardly wait. If you're
powerful enough, Karst, I may marry you."

They arrived at the movie and Karst bought
tickets.

Karst was eating popcorn. Esther was breathing
heavily. He inched away. Why had this strange girl
plunked herself into his life, he wondered. On the
screen Esther Blodgett was undergoing her metamor-
phosis into Vicky Lester. Suddenly it wasn't Esther-
Vicky; it was Faye Oppenheim he saw. And Karst, in
that second, paid silent tribute. While Janet Gaynor–
Blodgett–Lester broke every heart in the audience,
Faye Cassidy Oppenheim shimmered for him like an
eternal flame.

THURSDAY was publication day for Ulu Ubango's new book, and the Oppenheims were having a small dinner party for him.

Ubango, the New Zealand novelist, had written so searingly of his country's social strife that he was regarded by the literary elite as New Zealand's John Steinbeck. No doubt that when New Zealand's turn came to receive the Nobel Prize for literature, it would be Ubango's.

His publisher had brought Ubango to New York to meet the critics and promote his new book.

The lead review of the Sunday *New York Times* had called it a "flawed" masterpiece. A movie company had taken a year's option. Ubango's small but solid reputation was already palpitating the hearts of rival publishers.

Ubango was large and powerful. His shoulders were vast plains of muscle where one could slip into fantasy of original sin. Even the critics and editors standing in small, slouched groups felt a quickening pulse.

Gordon Oppenheim retrieved Ubango from some panting, wordy wives and drew him over to Claire Tuttle, a successful writer.

Claire was wearing a beaded headband. Her tousled red hair tumbled over it and onto a low, curved neckline. Her breasts appeared like crescent moons. Her smile, a glittering half moon, shined up at Ubango with wattage usually reserved for her appearances on Carson, Cavett and Frost.

"I have read her books," said Ubango. "She celebrates famous men."

"Oh, no," laughed Claire. "You've been taken in by the press. I fictionalize. Only fictionalize."

"What a pity," smiled Ubango. "There is so much more wickedness in truth."

Faye brought Paul Samuels over to meet Ubango. "This is Paul Samuels," she said. "Paul is my favorite Pulitzer author."

Ubango shook Samuels' hand, but his eye hit Faye and stuck there like flypaper. Faye, playing hostess, wandered to another group. He watched her gyrate across the floor, and he left Paul Samuels and Claire Tuttle to follow her.

Faye was standing near Gordon. She sensed Ubango behind her. His heavy breath was in her hair. He inhaled the tinted strands.

She turned toward him and asked, "Do you have a family?"

"Matrimony places emotional restraints on an artist. An artist must feel free."

"American writers are married and feel free."

"A marriage contract is like barbed wire. It pinches a writer's soul. I desire women but I do not desire a wife." He inhaled again. "Marvelous," he said.

Faye stood quietly during his inhalations. They felt like gentle puffs of wind.

"Inspiration! It is here," Ubango said suddenly.

"I could use some inspiration myself," Faye said.

"Inspiration flows from Mrs. Oppenheim like sap from a tree. A scent. An emission." He closed his eyes and held his breath. He was deathly still.

Faye thought that he might faint.

"Gracious Mrs. Oppenheim. In this sumptuous home, is there a quiet corner where we can enjoy a moment of privacy?"

"In my husband's study. We can be private there."

"Lead, lovely lady. I will follow."

Faye left the room. Ubango stalked her, observing every movement.

She entered the study and he shut the door behind them. He stood next to her and smelled. His breath pounded into her hair. He sniffed the air around her as though she were an exotic blossom. Seconds passed, moments, and still he sniffed. Then he placed his nose beside her and said, "Smelling the exterior of Mrs. Oppenheim no longer satisfies Ubango. He wishes to place his nose inside her delicate pink ear."

She sat quietly and he stuck his large, round nose into her lobe. They sat in perfect silence for five minutes and then he withdrew.

"Get up, please, Mrs. Oppenheim, and place yourself on my left."

Faye rose and moved over to the other side. He stuck his nose in her other ear. The only sound in the room was that of Ubango inhaling and exhaling, quietly at first, then spirited, until finally his breathing became so violent that Faye thought he had become ill.

He stopped. He withdrew his nose, thanked her and asked if she would spare him an extra precious few minutes.

Faye nodded and Ubango sat silently, regaining strength. Then he arose and without hesitation pressed his nose firmly between her loins. The hungry nose pressed upward. Its hard tip quivered. The wiry hairs in his nostril tickled her and she found it difficult to remain still. Faye found herself fighting desire. She began to ache.

Ubango's nose was grinding deeper. Its tip pushed upward like a mole burrowing toward the sun. A moist, mucous fluid drained down her leg. The nose darted from side to side. It uncovered strange new places that Faye hadn't realized existed. It found a cave and nuzzled in the warm hole. It scaled cliffs, descended depths, found fresh land and planted its stake.

Then the powerful body gathered energy and the nose exploded. A volcanic sneeze deep within her womb. The pressure eased. The nose inched back. It lingered for a final caress and withdrew.

"I have discovered America!" Ubango said and laid his head in her lap. They stayed together for another minute and then Ubango arose and said, "I must get back to my party. The critics will miss me." He brushed himself, looked into the mirror to examine his face, and left her.

Faye sat quietly in the empty room. She placed a finger on the tip of her mound. It was wet. Her finger followed the trail of the nose. It was soft, tender. The finger found the little cave. The cave was moist, damp. Suddenly Faye's body convulsed and the cave was at high tide. She pulled her finger out and smelled it. Musk. It was like sandalwood, rancid yet sweet. Faye took a deep breath and let it fill her lungs.

FAYE had always slept late while Gordon, up at seven, had his croissant and espresso, read his *Times* and walked to his office on Sixth Avenue to negotiate and administer the destiny of his writers. On one wall near his desk was framed: "Care less about Art, more about money." It was signed "George Bernard Shaw." Gordon cared for both. Talent warmed him like whiskey, and money gave him his sense of power. Every five years he reread *War and Peace*. It was his favorite book. He delighted in the blueprint of war and strategy. And during those occasional instances when he found himself floundering, he thought of the vagaries that can determine victory or loss in battle, and he forgave himself.

While Gordon went through his morning maneuvers, Faye had clung to her bed like a life raft. Occasionally she'd bolt into the bathroom to quell a shock of the dry heaves. Then she'd climb back into the soft, feathery warmth of her overstuffed bed, wondering how to get through the day.

Since publication of *The Big Bed* she had mastered bird watching, enrolled in a creative-writing workshop, studied nineteenth-century English Lit at the New School, cuisine with James Beard, run up staggering bills at every major department store, and caught the matinée of every movie released since 1962. Finally, exhausting the city's creative opportunities, she gave up on self-improvement and returned to bed. But now she was up with Gordon. They breakfasted together, and after Gordon left she turned to her typewriter.

The meetings with Paul Samuels were becoming spotty. She had written three chapters; the first was sensuous, the second repetitious, the third boring. Paul and Faye gave up on each other. Suddenly she felt the old emptiness, and when she woke up one morning with a return of the dry heaves, she decided to abandon her book.

"Gordon," she said over coffee, "it's over. I can't do it."

"Nonsense, Faye. Beginner's nerves. Give yourself a chance."

"I can't," she sobbed. "There's nothing to say."

"Faye," he said, in his soothing God voice, "all writers live with the fear that they've told it, their little tale. That they're all used up. Each one of them. That's why they become drunks and bullies. But it's only fear. Leave it alone for a few days. Buy a pretty dress. See a movie. I promise. It'll come." He gave her a light kiss, appropriated his briefcase and walked off to the wars.

Disconsolate, Faye went to bed. She thought about losing weight. Perhaps a week at a fat farm to lose the bloat. Maybe a story about a girl who couldn't stop eating. The idea bored her.

She slipped on a Cardin knit and took a taxi to Fifty-seventh Street. She looked in the windows of Bendel's. Mannequins in black matte jersey with silver-fox jackets dangling over one shoulder reminded her of a look she once had. She browsed through the downstairs boutiques, fingered a paisley shawl, a zebra boot, and waited for the up elevator.

She got out at Lingerie. Breathless, breastless ladies hovered over a display of wispy no-bras. Faye regarded her own full breasts with pride. A chic saleslady seemed preoccupied with air and held herself aloof from the sleek clientele. Faye glanced at some limp nighties hanging from a silver rack. She took a handful of size eights and went into one of the dressing rooms. She slipped into something satin. It gleamed like a pearl, close to her delicate, round body. Only her belly held any indication that sloth and indolence were nesting in her heart.

She scrutinized herself in the three-way mirror and in a lap-dissolve the image wavered and it was the early fifties. She saw a Faye Cassidy who spent her dimes and quarters on the latest *Silver Screen* and each new movie in town.

In a sudden hurdle from puberty to adolescence Faye was metamorphosed from a skinny, wistful kid into the sexpot of King City, California. She looked around her at the arid, cracked valleys and the barren scrubbed hills of the Salinas Valley, and then she slept with a rich farmer from a nearby town and borrowed fifty dollars to go to Hollywood and be a movie star.

She found a room on Ivar Street, a block away from Hollywood Boulevard, and hung around Central Casting. The offices were grimy and small, and Faye knew that the stairway to paradise would not ascend through these shabby doors.

John Digby, small-time ex-Broadway hustler, took a look at Faye and heard fate whistle. He asked her out to dinner. He leaned back in his chair, puffed his Tiparillo and said, "You're a damn pretty kid, Faye, but I tell you straight, you need T.A.P."

Faye looked at him trustingly.

"Take Monroe. She can't act her way out of a paper bag, but she's got it. Harlow, she had T.A.P. big. She could get a cock up like nobody else in town. Remember that, Faye, T.A.P."

"What is it?" Faye asked.

"Tits and Ass Power. You're dead in this town without it."

"T.A.P.? Is that like sex appeal?"

"Sex appeal was twenty years ago. Tits and Ass Power is now." He lifted his glass. "T.A.P.," he said. "Without it, you're nothing. With it, you got America by the balls."

Faye joined him in the toast. In a wavering voice she said, "Me for T.A.P."

That night she went to bed with John Digby and became his protégée. He kept assuring her that America was waiting. He made her bleach her hair platinum and lose ten pounds, and he sent her to a speech coach who lowered her register half an octave. She had plenty of Tits and Ass Power for John Digby. He spent half his business hours fucking her, but he couldn't seem to promote his own genital enthusiasm to the brass behind the studio doors.

One day he came home glowing. "The doors are opening, Fayzie. We're on our way." He'd arranged with some studio for a two-year contract at one hundred and fifty dollars a week.

He took her to Chasen's that night to celebrate. On the way to their table Digby stopped to talk to two Savile-Row–haberdashed men. He seemed to shrink as he introduced Faye to Mr. Lorenz, an RKO executive. Mr. Lorenz introduced them both to Gordon Oppenheim from New York.

Faye Cassidy wasn't as beautiful as Lombard,

sensuous as Monroe, or bouncy as Grable. Faye was trash. Gordon took one look at her and felt the same ecstatic thrill as in the closing of a six-figure business deal.

When Faye returned to her room on Ivar Street a few days later for a change of clothes, she found a dozen wilted roses on her doorstep. The enclosed card read:

Faye Cassidy:
   Meet me for dinner at eight. Call me at the Beverly Hills Hotel.

Gordon Oppenheim

Faye threw the dying roses into the garbage and dialed the hotel. "Is Mr. Oppenheim there?"

"Who's calling?"

"Faye Cassidy."

She was placed on hold and a moment later she heard Gordon's voice. "I expected to hear from you sooner."

"I was out of town on location."

"I'm leaving tomorrow. We'll have dinner tonight. Be here at eight."

"Yes, Mr. Oppenheim. I'll be there." She hung up and felt a heavy lassitude. She felt controlled by that voice as if it were a radar beam. If the voice said "Jump through the hoop for Gordon," she wondered if she would. She thought the voice might.

She washed her hair, massaged herself with Jer-

gens Lotion, and painted her finger and toe nails a
violent red.

John Digby picked her up and delivered her at
the hotel at eight-fifteen.

"Just be smart," he said. "Oppenheim knows everybody."

Her white satin dress was suspended by two thin
rhinestone straps. There was a slight stain near her
thigh. She walked to the house phone and asked for
Mr. Oppenheim.

"Who's calling, please?"

"Faye Cassidy."

Gordon sounded brusque.

"I'm sorry I'm late," Faye said. "I was working."

"I should have had a car pick you up. Come to
Bungalow Eight. We'll have dinner here."

Faye tripped along the foliaged path to Bungalow Eight. It was a small white stucco building with
oleander bushes and fuchsia shielding it from view.
Faye rang the bell.

She had to wait before Gordon opened the door.
He had on a navy velvet house jacket and expensive
slippers.

"I'm sorry I'm late," she repeated. "I was working."

"That's a bad habit," he said.

"I know, but I was working."

"That's a bad habit," he said again.

"Working?"

"No, lying. Lying is a bad habit for an ambitious

young girl." He smiled and his teeth suddenly seemed like shark's spikes. She wondered if he would nibble a bit first or swallow her whole.

"You don't mind some advice from a new friend," he added, cool and disinterested.

"Oh, no. I always welcome advice," she said, minding terribly.

"Your hair. It's awful! Change it."

"It can't be awful. It's T.A.P."

"What in hell is T.A.P.?" he asked.

"T.A.P. is Tits and Ass Power. You can't get anywhere in Hollywood without it."

He laughed delightedly. "Good God," he said, controlling his mirth. "Are they still feeding you that pigshit? This Digby, is he your guiding light?"

"John Digby is my manager," she said loyally.

"I'll bet he is. What'd he get you, a two-year contract at one fifty a week?"

"How do you know that?" she gasped.

"Your hair. Your shoes."

"Can I sit down?"

"Of course."

She gyrated across the room and eased into a chair as if she were squeezed out of a tube. "What's wrong with my shoes?"

"They throw your balance. You lurch."

She sat gracefully, and in a controlled effort to protect the interests of Tits and Ass Power, she asked, "Is that why no man can resist looking when I come into a room? Is that why you sent flowers after just

making my acquaintance?" She felt she'd scored her
first goal.

"They're not looking at you, Miss Cassidy, they're
conjuring up a stag movie."

"So *that's* your business, Mr. Oppenheim!"

"Staggies?" He laughed again. "I deal in million-
dollar product. That's why I like you."

Faye Cassidy, America's hottest teen-age kid
from King City, California, said, "I suppose women
are different in New York. But this is Hollywood and
Mr. Digby has worked here for more than twenty
years, so I guess he knows more about things here
than someone from three thousand miles away, even
in million-dollar product."

Gordon was very quiet. Gently he said, "You're a
pretty girl, Faye. I like you. You're uneducated, but
you're loyal. You have spirit. Maybe you have talent.
But Mr. Digby is a two-bit flesh peddler. Sure, he got
you a job. You're a sexy kid. The studio boys'll think
you vibrate. *You* think they'll make you a star. But
what's likely is that you'll 'render service.' They'll
send you out to be Miss Dairy Queen of Iowa. They'll
squire you around with some new actor they're pro-
moting. Maybe one'll take a fancy and fuck you.
Maybe you'll get a walk-on. They'll dress you. They'll
feed you. And, Miss Cassidy, they will own you. Is
that what you want?"

"I want to be a movie star."

Gordon laughed. "What color's your hair?"

"It's blond."

"Digby make you bleach it?"

"I photograph much better now."

"How do you know?"

"Mr. Digby's gotten me a screen test."

"You see it?"

"He told me."

"What else has he told you?"

"He told me I could be a movie star."

"What did you say?"

"I said yes, of course! Listen, why am I here?"

"What else did he do?"

"He's introducing me to studio talent executives. He knows people at all the studios."

"I'll bet he does!"

"What does that mean?"

"It means if you're a smart little girl you'll dye your hair back. You are no Monroe, Miss Cassidy, and that chippy look won't make you one. Then you will go and tell Mr. Digby that you don't like his style of flesh peddling and that he should go fuck himself. And then it means that you will listen to me.

"It means that you can also be a very dumb little girl. It means you can go back to Digby and let him sell you to the studios for another five years. It means they might try to make you into some cheap imitation of Monroe or Novak or whoever in hell they have in mind, and whoever it is, Miss Cassidy, you are lost. Finished. Dead. You'll have to do everything they want, whatever the hell it is. And if you don't . . . if you say no, it means they'll suspend you. And

that means they still own you but they don't have to
pay you. And that's about the best your Digby can get
for you."

Faye sat quietly and listened. She felt over-
whelmed by Gordon Oppenheim. She felt she could
become his thing, his object; that he might slip her
into his pocket like a watch fob. She realized that if
the studios didn't own her, Gordon Oppenheim would.
"Why are you telling me all this?"

"You interest me."

Why should she interest Gordon Oppenheim?
She figured it was her terrific Tits and Ass Power.

"You remind me of something from the past. You
know, Faye, I've always had a soft spot for the twenties. I collect first editions. Books. I own first editions
of every major writer in the twenties. I don't know
what in hell it is, but you're like something from
Fitzgerald."

"Who's he?"

A flush of horror passed through him, but Gordon
said patiently, "The first thing you need is an education. I'm going to send you some books. Read them.
Do nothing but read them. That's all. Read."

She raised her sumptuous bosom.

"Do everything I tell you. Read everything I send
you. You'll end up in a duplex penthouse with a tiara
on your head." Then he kissed her softly on her lips
and she felt an enormous erection pushing its way
toward heaven.

As FAYE regarded her body through Bendel's three-way mirror, she noticed that her once sinewy curves now strained the satin gown to its seams.

Never a star! Even with that heavenly body, I would never have been a movie star. Gordon knew that. Gordon saved me. I owe him my life. She sighed regretfully. I owe Gordon everything.

What next? Faye didn't know. She only knew it had to be something.

She slipped out of the shiny gown, and opening her letter-size Gucci bag, she tucked it in, along with another sliver of chiffon. Her purse barely snapped shut.

A fifty-fifty chance, she decided.

She picked up the rejects with her free hand and sauntered casually into the salesroom. Salesladies were still unconcerned with customers, but small clerks in dark dresses appeared like gnomes to retrieve the discarded lingerie. Faye left the nightgowns on a counter and waited with faint fatigue for an elevator. She left the store and stepped to the curb to hail a cab when a plump man of about forty-five approached her.

"Excuse me, madam," he said tentatively, "but I've been notified that you haven't returned all the merchandise. I'd like to examine your pocketbook, please."

"Me?" Faye said pleasantly.

"Yes, ma'am. I'd like to look in your bag."

"You're making a mistake," Faye said. "I'm Mrs. Gordon Oppenheim. I've been a charge customer here for over fifteen years."

"Sorry, ma'am. I'm obliged to look."

Faye moistened her curvy lips. "How old are you?" she asked softly.

"I'd like your bag, Mrs. Oppenheim."

"Rotten luck," Faye said. "Having to spy on women all day long."

"Look here, ma'am!"

"I suppose you've been at it for years. What do they pay you, a hundred and fifty a week?"

"I hate to get rough, ma'am, but you just keep on—"

"See that building?" Faye said, pointing through a splinter of space. "My husband's office is on the thirty-third floor. My husband makes one hundred and fifty dollars an hour. Isn't that sad—no," she interrupted herself, "just plain bad luck that one man makes in an hour what another makes in a forty-hour week."

"Lady, I don't give a damn what your husband makes. I see a lot of rich spoiled broads."

"I'll bet you do. Year in, year out. What a way to pass a life."

"I want that purse!"

"I didn't get your name, mister, but cops, even plain-clothes men, store detectives like yourself, are very much in demand, very hot this year."

"Lady, I'm gonna hafta book you if you don't cooperate."

"*The French Connection,* an Oscar, three cop stories scheduled to start shooting this year, two nonfiction best sellers by cops, every studio in town, every publishing house has a cop and is making a deal with him."

The store detective stared nervously at his suspect. "You a reporter or something?"

"What's your name? I'll tell you everything."

"LaCicco. Richard LaCicco."

"Mr. LaCicco. This is the year of the pig. Robert
Redford, Al Pacino, Jack Nicholson, they're all crazy
to play cops. And here you are wasting your life as
a spy in ladies' lingerie."

"I'm a detective, Mrs. Oppenheim, and I'm proud
of my work. And this ain't getting you off the hook.
So open that purse."

Jail or bed? Faye weighed the alternatives.

"Mrs. Oppenheim, I'm going to have to report
you."

She saw herself passing sleepless nights on a
straw mattress, roaches and rats running between her
legs and breasts. She felt the ridicule heaped on her,
a rich spoiled liberal, by honest, hard-working crooks.
Repressed lesbians crawling over her like ants. Sadis-
tic matrons molesting her, beating her, shaving her
head. Isolation and despair. Barred windows, watery
gruel. A montage of Warner Bros. prison brutality
spliced itself into her life. And she knew that Gordon
would have a gaggle of lawyers at the police station
faster than it took Ruth Snyder to fry—so jail was
out.

"Silly man," she said coyly. "I did. I took them."

"Then I'll have to—"

She grinned ingenuously, exquisitely, and La-
Cicco felt his heart beat. He stared in bewilderment
as Mrs. Oppenheim was metamorphosed into Faye
Cassidy. She looked like a perishable dream. He
reached out to touch her.

"Not here," she said. "Not now." She took his arm and guided him across the street.

LaCicco, befuddled by this blond apparition, let himself be led away.

"Dear man," she was saying, "why throw your life away squinting through peepholes when you too might have a profitable literary career."

"I'm a cop," he said, holding on. "And, besides, I can't spell."

She beamed at him. "Spelling is what bright young editors do. We'll have lunch at the Plaza and talk the whole thing over."

Good afternoon, Mrs. Oppenheim," said the maître d', greeting her at the entrance to the Oak Room.

"A table for two," Faye said.

"*Oui, madame.*" He turned and led them down the aisle. Faye waved jauntily to Michael Stone. He was sitting alone.

"Who's that?" LaCicco asked.

"Michael Stone. He got a National Book Award a few years ago. He's not a very good writer, but he's handsome and very American. So the ladies on the jury gave it to him."

"What's wrong with that?" asked LaCicco sullenly.

Faye burst into a smile. She waved happily at an attractive redhead walking toward Stone.

"Who's she?"

"Claire Tuttle. She's meeting him, and that makes me happy. It means they're both hard at work. They will have new books by fall. My husband will sell their books for a great deal of money. And I can buy a new tiara."

"Look, Mrs. Oppenheim. Why exactly do you steal? You know these famous people. You must be loaded. I don't get it about you broads. Does it get you hot or something?"

"I *steal to meet you.*" Faye waved across the room. "They're wondering who's my mystery man."

"What do you mean they're hard at work? How can they be at one of the fanciest places in town and be hard at work?"

Faye stretched her leg across his thigh. "They're writers. She writes books about sex and romance. He writes books about sex and romance. And this is where they do their research."

"That ain't such a bad way of earning a living."

"You bet. A rich and satisfying life. She's more satisfied than he because she's richer. She's richer because she writes faster."

They finished their cold salmon salad and Faye

flashed him a "let's get the hell upstairs" look. Her eyes were bright as sunspots.

He was quiet. He felt her leg rocking against his thigh. It burned through his trousers. "I don't think you're a bad person, Mrs. Oppenheim. Maybe those things got stuck in your purse by accident."

"You've made me very happy." Her leg stopped as she signaled for the waiter. She signed the tab and they left the restaurant.

She went to the front desk and booked a room. They followed the bellboy who led them to the eighth floor. He discretely showed them the empty closets, the disinfected bathroom and the air conditioner. La-Cicco reluctantly gave him a quarter.

Faye slipped off her Cardin knit. She wore lace bikini underpants but no brassiere. "If I was a whore, Richard, would you fuck me or book me?"

He turned away for privacy, unzipped himself and stepped out of his trousers. He folded them in their crease and put them on a hanger.

As he turned toward Faye she saw that his cock had already peeked from his crumpled white shorts. He slid them off and it flew to half mast. "I'd fuck you and then I'd book you," he said, reaching for her.

"You'd be my accomplice," she said.

"They'd never believe I'd fucked you. After all, I'm a cop."

She giggled. He kissed her with lips that felt like bricks. His body was soft. It seemed disconnected from him. His cock probed at her clitoris, and barely managing penetration, he came in short spasmodic throbs.

She pushed him off and went to the window. The city looked warm and active as if life were out *there,* beckoning.

What am I doing with this shmuck? It made no sense. He looked like a seal, slippery and damp. She felt like speared bait.

He puffed himself up and walked over to her.

"Show me a hooker," she said.

"In my line of business, you get to be a woman specialist—all women got *some* hooker in 'em." He gave her a knowing look. "By the way, that writer stuff you were telling me about . . . How do I do it?"

"Take them to bed like you did me."

"I didn't take you. You took me."

"Keep notes. Tell the ladies you won't press charges when you catch them shoplifting. All they have to do is give you information. Write it down. Don't worry about the spelling. When you have enough pages, you look up paperback publishers in the classified section of the telephone book. If the publisher likes it, he will probably give you a couple of thousand dollars. You're in a very privileged position, you know." She looked at LaCicco and sighed. How Gordon would love to find a new Hammett come over the transom.

LaCicco listened carefully. Then, thoughtfully, he asked, "And why do you do what it is you do?"

"I am rehabilitating myself. At one time I was a

movie star. I gave up my career to marry a rich man. I have a laundress, a housekeeper and a cleaning man. I have nothing to do. I was becoming a wreck. My husband urged me to shape up. I promised him I would. I am rehabilitating myself to make my husband happy. People who write books make my husband happy. Unfortunately, since I have nothing to say, I must invent a new life. You are simply a little moment in my new life."

LaCicco looked at Faye with interest.

"You, on the other hand, are surrounded by life. Women stealing for pleasure, secretly wishing discovery, desiring punishment. You are in the middle of, uh, the pulse of life."

"Hey, I like that, *The Pulse of Life.*"

"See, you've got your title." She felt rage against Gordon. What in hell am I talking paperback advances with a fat cop who ejaculates before he's half in? Why was Gordon pushing her into *The Pulse of Life* with this fat cop?

"How do I know it'll sell?" asked LaCicco, already a hungry writer.

She thought with affection of her old low-grade depressions.

"*The Pulse of Life,*" he said. "I like that. Look, I'm not going to report you this time, Mrs. Oppenheim, but I suggest you give up this life. I'd hate to see a lady like you end up a hardened criminal."

GORDON OPPENHEIM was
in love with his office. It
sat on the thirty-third floor of a Sixth Avenue money
palace. The furniture was custom-made, the floors car-
peted in overlapping antique rugs.

His hobby was first editions of American writers
of the 1920s. His shelves held copies of *The Great
Gatsby, The Sun Also Rises, The Green Hat, You
Can't Go Home Again.* His first editions were like a
talisman. They seemed to insure that Gordon Oppenheim dealt in quality goods.

He was surrounded by his writers. To the west he could see his Jews into satire and black comedy; his headstrong Irishmen pushing past the Jews to stamp their own sensibility on the publishing psyche.

Over on the east were his blockbusters, his story-tellers with five-hundred-thousand-dollar advances before the publisher even saw a word.

He kept an eye peeled across the East River into Brooklyn, for who knew when another Thomas Wolfe would walk across the waters. He listened for the D train from the Bronx: Waiting for Weidman.

He had a sixth sense for talent. He ferreted it out, signed it up, encouraged it, and unswervingly got it the best deal in town.

Part neuter, part heterosexual, it was the six-figure deal he felt in his crotch. A movie sale with a piece of the gross straight off the top was a hurricane beating through his body like a primeval force. This was his true sexual energy.

CLAIRE TUTTLE was having lunch with Gordon at the Italian Pavilion. Claire arrived early and was ushered by the maître d' to Gordon's usual table. She understood immediately why Gordon preferred table nineteen. It was detached, insuring privacy, yet from its central position he could survey the entire room. Red incandescent lights gave it the glow of soft coals. One could talk business in an atmosphere as intimate as a bedroom. Claire analyzed the clientele as she waited.

She recognized a few writers, an old editor of hers, the cool, prestigious agents in tweed laughing at threadbare jokes of young editors eager for important authors. There was much gossiping by young women working for magazines and movie companies. They depended on each other for tips, incidental information which might result in an early look at a manuscript.

The Pavilion was an offshoot of the book business. It was a publishing *La Ronde*. Everyone knew everyone else and would be playing the same game the following week.

Claire was a prolific commercial author. She wrote about her love affairs and she wrote about her friends' love affairs. She was a celebrity collector and her heroes were movie stars, politicians, revolutionaries or authors more prestigious than herself. She wrote in a crisp, simple style. Her books were romantic and her publisher called her a "good read."

She complained everlastingly about how poor she was, but her books were translated into twenty-six languages, paperback sales often fell into six figures, and three books had been bought for the movies. She had done a screen adaptation of a best-selling novel but she was fired after the first draft. From this experience, however, she'd written her Hollywood novel. It never sold to the movies but it had over a million sales in paperback.

She had been married but her husband had left her. She had written a thinly disguised version of an extramarital affair she was having at the time. "How could you do this to me?" he had wailed.

"I invent everything," she said. "I only create. My beloved, would I lie to you?"

He believed her and stayed with her until her next novel, in which he recognized his best friend as her lover. He ranted. He raved. He screamed. "Sneak! How could you use me so?"

"It's all made up!" she sobbed.

This time he had her. In Claire's haste to deliver the manuscript, she had failed to disguise her cuckolded husband, and he found himself reading descriptions of their most intimate moments together, word-perfect.

"It's a nervous tic," he wailed. "Whenever you make love with me, my partner, my best friend, you write it down. Nothing is sacred. You don't even let the sheets dry in your haste to make the fall list."

He stayed in the house for a few weeks, typing her long farewells, then destroying them, fearful of seeing them in print. Then one day he packed his bags and left. He left Claire a one-line note that he hoped she couldn't do much with.

Claire:
   You've used me up. I'm hanging on to what's left.
                              Don

Claire became melancholy. She had loved Don. She pined. She grieved. Listless, she stayed away from the typewriter. She cried at night and woke up in the morning, shaking. She was profoundly sad.

Then one afternoon Don came back to pick up some lapis lazuli cuff links that he'd left behind. It was a gray day with a high pollution index. The windows in the apartment were open and a sensuous fog filled the rooms. Claire had on a transparent caftan robe and her breasts bubbled as she walked. Her hair had grown during her grief and it tumbled loosely over her opulent breasts. Don looked at her as though she were a Rubens. He felt a wild thrill. Had he been unjust? Had his accusations stemmed from jealousy of her success?

Claire looked at Don with innocent dark eyes. She whispered despairingly, "I still love you."

"I came for my lapis cuff links," he said.

"They're in the bedroom," she said.

He followed her into their bedroom. It was strewn with newspapers and magazines. The bed looked as if it had been made by a six-year-old. It was lopsided and full of bumps. Her notebooks were closed. They were covered with dust.

"I'm miserable," she said.

"Don't!" Don said manfully. He felt a curious pride. His leaving had stopped Claire from working.

"I can't live without you," Claire said. She slipped off the caftan. She stood in the polluted mist and Don felt his penis grow six feet. He made love to her, and afterward, as she lay in his arms, she said, "Please come back. Make me a woman again."

"Let's think about it," Don said coolly. "Let's consider it." He felt terrific *machismo*.

Don left the house full of admiration. He felt proud of his resistance and his diplomacy. He felt admiration for Claire. She was an expert in bed, a talented writer with a hunger for life. The longer he thought about it the more he felt he'd misjudged her. After all, Claire was an artist, and artists were different. They had to look to life for material. They regarded experience differently from others. He went to his hotel and thought about going back to Claire.

He thought about it the next day and the day after that. Then he received a note from Claire:

> My Love,
> I cannot live without you.
> Claire

Don felt dizzily happy. He had always pursued Claire. He had lived in the shadow of her success. He didn't call Claire that day or the next. This time she must really want him.

Instead, he called a friend of Claire's. He took her friend to dinner and afterward he made love to her. It wasn't very good and he found himself thinking of Claire.

"You still love Claire," her friend said.

Don was silent.

Days passed, and Don received another note from Claire:

Darling,
I am chaste. Relieve my pain.

Claire

Don grew philosophical. No decent woman would have an affair with her husband's best friend and write a book about it. He grinned at his own narcissism. He smiled at his pained vanity. Imagine, a husband seeing his own image in each of his wife's books. He felt happy with his new humility and decided to return to Claire.

The next day he called Claire's friend and took her out to dinner. Afterward Don said, "Let's walk home." He put his arm through hers and they sauntered uptown.

"I spoke to Claire today," her friend said. "I told her I was seeing you tonight."

"What did she say?" Don asked.

"She asked me not to go to bed with you."

"What did you say?"

"I said I wouldn't."

Don felt marvelous. Under no circumstances would he go to bed with Claire's friend. Yet, he was unfettered. He was free. Why shouldn't he go to bed with Claire's friend, sow a last oat before returning to Claire. Or should he return to Claire in trust, a weekend virgin.

"I think I'm going to go back to Claire," he said.

"I'm glad," her friend said. "She loves you."

"Claire's lucky to have such a good friend," Don

said. "I'd like to think of you as my friend too."

Claire's friend squeezed his arm in comradeship.

Don left her at her Seventy-second Street apartment. "You'll be the first to know," he said.

Weeks passed and still Don stalled. He did not call Claire or Claire's friend. He worked hard at the office and spent the evenings seeing double features on Forty-second Street. One night after work he stopped at the newsstand to buy a paper and noticed Claire's name on the new *Cosmo*. He bought a copy and went back to his hotel to read it.

THE CUFF LINKS
by Claire Tuttle

The first sentence read: "It had been an awful year. Corinne and Bill knew it was time to separate." Then the story went on to recount how Bill returns to the apartment to retrieve his lapis lazuli cuff links which he'd left behind. Aroused by the beautiful Corinne, Bill makes love to her.

It was a short, erotic story, but it contained in detail the events of that gray, polluted afternoon.

"Cunt!" Don screamed. "She's done it again."

Quickly he phoned Claire's friend. "This is Don," he said.

"Yes," the friend said coolly.

"Remember the last time we had dinner?"

"Of course."

"Remember you told me that you had talked to Claire?"

"Yes."

"What did you tell her?"

"I told you."

"Tell me again."

"She asked me not to go to bed with you."

"That's all she said?"

"The usual chitchat."

"What usual chitchat? What usual chitchat?"

"You're repeating yourself."

"Tell me everything in detail," he said.

"Who can remember?" Don waited. "Well, Claire was pretending it was all a lark."

"Oh, my God," Don moaned.

"What's the matter?"

"Did you tell her anything about us?"

"What do you mean?"

"You know what I mean."

"You mean making it together? No."

"You're sure?"

"She already knew."

"*She knew!* How could she know?"

"I'd already told her."

"How could you? Oh, my God, when did you do that?"

"She called me the day after it happened. Claire intuits things. She wasn't angry, though."

"And you just told her?"

"It just came out. She seemed so amused by the fact that we'd both gone to bed with you that I thought that you'd already told her."

"That bitch!" Don said. "Well, I hope you're amused when you read all about it in this month's *Cosmo.*"

"What are you talking about?"

"Her tic! Claire's tic. My God, she's done it again. And I was going back to that slut." Don hung up and lay on his bed.

He thought about Claire and her insatiable habit of recording everything. She was like a junkie except that instead of a needle she'd reach for a pencil. He thought of her friends, her writer friends. Were they all like that? Did they share that compulsive urge to put it all down, each sordid, squalid detail of their lives? He began to calculate the money they made by fucking. A prostitute made from twenty to fifty dollars a trick, but some writers made a hundred thousand dollars a book. And some books reached only one climax, like *Marjorie Morningstar.* How much had Herman Wouk made on that one? And Norman Mailer. Or Philip Roth. On masturbation alone he'd made a two-hundred-and-fifty-thousand-dollar movie sale.

And Christ, Claire. If he took her books, fuck by fuck, and added up the royalties! The injustice of it made him shudder.

He felt a sudden love and compassion for all prostitutes. He yearned to run out into the streets to find one and tell her her inequities. He wanted to show her how she could quadruple her measly earnings by writing it down, each squalid, humiliating experience. He had to physically control himself from running amuck through the dark empty streets of New York looking for trade.

What a racket, he thought bitterly. What a goddamn racket.

A dim and distant idea teetered along somewhere inside him, and then, like an unbridled tornado, it smashed right into the frontal lobe of his brain. Suddenly Don Tuttle, foolish cuckolded husband of successful blabbermouth novelist Claire Tuttle, saw a way to capitalize on that world which had made life so painful for him, publishing. It could be done with fucking, scandal or murder. The possibilities were infinite. He thought of Truman Capote recording the disorderly death of the Clutter family, grossing millions before the murderers were executed. And hitting the best-seller list, with a movie to boot.

Don Tuttle would become the Sherlock Holmes of squalor. He would seek out victims, urge and encourage them to record their filthy, low lives. With luck, a Jackie Susann might arise like a phoenix from the dregs.

He picked up the phone and called Claire's friend.

"Don," she apologized, "I didn't mean to betray you."

"Betray?" he cried joyfully. "All's forgiven. But I need your help."

"What can I do?" she said abjectly.

"Quit your crummy job."

"But I like my work."

"Like! How can you like a job . . . Think! Think

very carefully. How was I? I mean, what was I really like?"

"I don't get it."

"How did it feel fucking your best friend's husband?"

"Donald!"

"I won't take it personally. But was I lousy? Remember every detail. Then try to remember every fuck you've ever had, with who and where. Then meet me tomorrow at the Italian Pavilion and we'll talk about an advance against your first novel."

GORDON OPPENHEIM sauntered behind the maître d' to his table. "Sorry I'm late, Claire. Call from London." He sat beside her and kissed her cheek. He noticed that she had already ordered a drink, so he ordered a Campari and soda and turned his rapt attention toward her.

"I've just finished your manuscript, and it's brilliant! Brilliant!"

"I think it's my best work, Gordon."

"Brilliant, absolutely."

"I'm glad you agree with me, Gordon."

"We may have one little problem, Claire. I think you should be aware of it."

"What problem, Gordon?"

"Libel."

"But Gordon, darling, you know I invent all my characters. It's all fiction."

"Of course, Claire. You know it. I know it. It's just an unintentional similarity to that ghastly Langdon person."

"My dear Gordon. Alan Langdon had ten wives. Seven of his ten wives were celebrated lesbians. My hero has only six wives, of which only four are lesbians, and two bisexual at that. There's no similarity at all."

"Darling, the publisher is letting his lawyer take a look. We must be sure there's no possibility that Langdon gets a notion you've even thought of him."

"Gordon, word of honor, I've never even met Langdon."

"Just protection, Claire. But I loved it. Marvelous. Literary Guild is bound to pick it up, and I see a marvelous movie in it. What a part! If only Brando were younger."

Claire seemed distracted.

"What is it, Claire darling?"

"Gordon, I'm so excited by my next book."

He nodded respectfully.

"I'm a little frightened by it. It's new. A metaphor for sex."

"Sounds abstract," he said.

"An artist must stretch."

Gordon thought of the plummeting sales but he kept a fixed smile.

Claire's expression suddenly clouded. "That prick!"

Don Tuttle entered the room. He waved to Gordon and Claire from across the room. The maître d' led him to a table where two young women were waiting.

"Don's into greener pastures," Claire said coldly.

"He's a natural," Gordon said. "He's got a sixth sense for a chatty clitoris."

"I notice you send him a writer or two." She smiled bitterly.

"Well, Claire, there is an audience for that. Writers must eat too."

"To think I let him penetrate my body." Claire shuddered.

"Claire, darling. You must take Don's success with some humor. He gives you full credit. Says you're completely responsible."

"Shit!"

"Michael Stone's new book is in. It's quite marvelous. Let me send you galleys," said Gordon, hoping to distract her.

Claire suddenly seemed radiant. "I do love Michael," she said. Her manner improved instantly, and Gordon and Claire passed a pleasant hour gossiping and discussing advances and royalties.

GET anything done?" Gordon asked a few days later.

"Fiddling around."

"I know how hard it is to get started. Stick with it. It'll come."

"Gordon, how can I make you believe me. I truly have nothing to write about."

"Claire Tuttle—do you think Claire has something to say?"

"She's a walking tribute to Krafft-Ebing. Is that what you want from me?"

"Faye, you've boxed yourself in. Take a fresh look! New York City! You're living in the pulse of life!"

Faye groaned as she remembered LaCicco.

"For God's sake, you must have felt something in fifteen years. What about motherhood? What about marriage?"

"Gordon, I was not a sociologist keeping a daily survey on a declining marriage."

Gordon wasn't listening. His brilliant sense of the market was adjusting itself to Faye's predicament. "A great beauty fades into obscurity. At thirty-five she feels that life has passed her by. *The Crisis of an Aging Beauty!*" he said excitedly. "*Ladies' Home Journal* will love it."

Faye looked at her husband skeptically. "You really are serious, aren't you?"

He nodded, and she noticed affection in his eyes.

"Very well, Gordon," she sighed. "I will keep on trying."

MICHAEL STONE had left Stratford Avenue in the Bronx with the complete works of Hemingway in his trunk. At Harvard he took a leap into the Romantics and emerged from the dark waters of the nineteenth century with an English accent, a skill at fencing and a love of Feudal Glory. While Michael now talked with an English accent, he seduced sounding Southern and he screwed sounding Black. He was soon the desire of every Radcliffe freshman.

He came across Annabelle Ornitz's poems in the *Harvard Advocate*. They were melancholy poems, and he wrote asking to meet her. Annabelle was a virgin when she met Michael. She abandoned herself to him, and afterward in her room she played Schubert. Annabelle loved Schubert. She played "Death and the Maiden" and she fell into an intense depression. She mistook her depression to be ecstasy, to be love for Michael Stone. She saw them passing poetic years together. She imagined a passionate conjugal life with the boy from the Bronx.

She knew of his reputation. She'd heard tales of his erotic powers. But she had a good heart and she felt that she could bind him to her through devotion and fidelity. She thought, One day he will be mine.

She wrote wild and tortured poems about her love. They were published in *Poetry Magazine*. She began to enjoy a small success as a poet. Michael was impressed. Most of the 'cliffies would become researchers, editors, marry into the Establishment. But Annabelle, well, Annabelle could blossom into another Edna St. Vincent Millay. He knew that she was aware that he had other girls, but her patience and her silence led him to think that he loved her. She was true. He was a greedy fellow and he would need a woman of stoic good will. All she wanted was Michael Stone and Poetry. He believed that. It satisfied him.

On graduation Annabelle received a Fulbright and went to Rome for a year. She wrote Michael ardent letters which he kept in a shoe box.

He went to New York, got a job in a publishing house, but became immensely bored. He felt superior to his authors and he started making notes for his own novel. He was fired. He lived on unemployment and plunged into work. He wrote in a frenzy. He was white heat. He met a lady agent who was impressed with his gifted body, and she took him on as a client.

Weeks later she called him excitedly and told him that she had sold *Women and Strangers* for five thousand dollars and she thought it a cinch for serialization. That night he fucked the lady agent. They lay awake till morning talking deals. Michael said he wanted to write the screenplay. The agent said, "Take the money and run." Later that day he wrote Annabelle and asked her to marry him.

Annabelle came home to Michael. They were married and they were happy. Annabelle kept a quiet, orderly house so that Michael could work, and she cooked small dinner parties for editors, publishers and critics.

Michael's energetic agent sold his book to the movies and Michael flew to Hollywood to consult with the producers. Consultations were restricted to breakfasts and lunches, meals that stretched out for hours. The air grew heavy. The drinking dried Michael out. No one made a decision. At night he was alone. He dreamed wistfully of Hollywood parties and wondered where they were. He called Annabelle four times a day, loved her madly in absentia and yearned to get home.

One day the producer brought his girl to lunch. She was a luscious young blonde named Faye Cassidy. The producer shared her with her agent, Digby, an ex-Broadway gossip columnist.

Michael Stone and Faye Cassidy took one look at each other and it spelled out *HEATHCLIFF AND CATHY.* They languished over daiquiris in the Polo Lounge, they walked the shabby Pacific beaches. And then, one mournful afternoon, while the sun was glowing in the west, the producer came home early. He found Michael and Faye clenched tightly in his bed. Agents were one thing, writers another. Michael went home to Annabelle to start his novel on Hollywood, and Faye disappeared up beyond the Sunset Strip into the shadowy protection of Digby.

Annabelle, now more housewife than poet, was still listening to Schubert. But her tears no longer fell for her Jewish Prince, but for her own grieving heart. She knew of his infidelities. They were legend. She set her mind on being a good wife, thought of salvation and waited. She was patient, pious and numb. Occasionally a vision of revenge filtered into her consciousness, like sunlight into a prison cell, but she blocked it out. She remained stoic. One day his energies would wane. One day. She went back to her poems as a substitute for Michael, published them, and this relieved slightly the pain that was becoming a small hard knot of gastric anxiety.

Their only life together was at the movies. Michael loved Fred Astaire. He loved Cary Grant. And above all, he loved Errol Flynn. In the darkened movie house, Michael felt happy. Tears fell on his cheek, and Annabelle, for these few moments, felt peace. Michael was hers now. An emotional little boy crying his heart out at all those sad celluloid lives.

ONE spring morning the phone rang and a frail, small voice asked for Michael.

"Who is it?" asked Annabelle.

"Esther Oppenheim. Can I speak to your husband, please? It's important."

Annabelle knocked on Michael's door. "Working?" she asked.

He nodded.

"Oppenheim's girl is on the phone. Says it's important."

Michael picked up the dusty receiver. "Yes?" he said.

"Mr. Stone, this is Esther Oppenheim. I know you're working, but I need a favor."

"What?"

"Hard to explain now. Could you meet me after school just a few minutes?"

"I'm afraid n—" Michael hesitated, looked at the sentence he'd been stuck with all morning. "All right," he said. "Where's your school?"

"Ninetieth and Park. Three-fifteen. This afternoon?"

"Okay." He hung up.

"What does she want?" Annabelle asked.

"Don't know. Oppenheim told her to call."

Annabelle gave him a suspicious look and left him alone.

MICHAEL was there at three-fifteen. Little girls tumbled by, holding hands and hugging each other. He regarded this prepubescent world with happiness. It was so tender and fresh. They were like fawns and small sweet animals. A pretty girl detached herself from the others and approached him.

"Thank you for coming, Mr. Stone."

"My God!" Michael said, dumbstruck. "You look just like your mother."

"She said you were an old friend."

"Your mother said that?"

"She said she introduced you to Daddy."

Michael recalled it was because of Faye that he'd left the lady agent with a taste for sinewy genius and gone to Gordon.

"Mother said you were a Romantic."

Michael looked at Esther's golden hair and re-called a boyhood predilection for Iseult the Fair.

"We're studying medieval history and I thought an awareness of the heroes and the poetry would make the period more personal."

"Let's walk through the park," he said. "By the time we hit Central Park West you'll be an au-thority."

"No," Esther said. "Let's rent a car and drive to the sea."

Michael found the girl intriguing and they went to a nearby Hertz and soon were on their way.

He took the East River Drive toward the Tri-borough Bridge. Traffic was light and they roared along pleasantly.

Michael drove along in silence. Occasionally a dark expression crossed his face. He turned, glanced at Esther and remembered Faye Cassidy when she was a young blond starlet. Esther lacked her mother's wanton sensuality. She was vulnerable, almost raw. An easy prey for love. He would have to be careful.

He thought proudly of the hordes of women he'd known. His victories were catalogued and cross-indexed in a locked filing cabinet in his workroom. Yet lately he'd felt a lassitude, a curious lack of desire.

Suddenly, driving along with the daughter of his first Hollywood blonde, he surrendered to art. Life is a circle, he thought. He scrutinized her. The young girl became intensely important.

He wandered off to the memorable fantasies of his life; like a movie before him he saw Heathcliff and Cathy, Héloïse and Abélard, Tristan and Iseult. Something, a tear, passed through his eye.

Michael's brooding silence intrigued Esther. "Are you ill, Mich—"

Suddenly he burst out into song. His froggy baritone hit the wind like a 727.

> *"So sturben wir,*
> *um ungetrennt*
> *ewig einig,*
> *ohne Eng'*
> *Ohn' Erwachen,*
> *Ohn' Erbangen*
> *Namenlos*
> *in Lieb' umfangen*
> *ganz uns selbst gegeben,*
> *der Liebe nur zu leben."*

"Wagner's *Tristan and Iseult*, love duet, Act Two, scene two," he said fastidiously.

Esther looked at him shyly. She felt her choice a success. He was handsome, a National Book Award

winner and an ardent Romantic. The doors to life
would finally open.

They passed the suburban split-level houses that
lead toward Jones Beach, each in his own small dream.
Esther was finally to know love. Michael was to span
a generation. First Faye, now Esther. Biological juices
rushed into his prick. He felt like Galsworthy as the
first chapter began to lay itself out.

They arrived at the beach and Michael parked in
a deserted lot. They walked along like young lovers.
A few stragglers were leaving, returning to their cars
and the city, but Michael and Esther walked against
the wind onto the sand.

She took off her shoes and Michael thought of
Dietrich straggling behind Gary Cooper in *Morocco*.
For a second, Jones Beach was every bit as exotic as
the Sahara.

Esther was anxious. Would he love her? What
would she feel? Would it hurt?

They walked along for about a mile and Michael
said, "Here, we'll stop here."

The beach was deserted. No one was to be seen.
They sat watching the waves lap the shore. The sun
began its slow descent and Michael reached over and
pulled Esther to him. He hugged her keen young
body and he remembered her mother. The girl was
smaller than Faye but she would develop. Her arms
were already shapely and her breasts were like pink
sea shells. He pulled up her dress. She smelled like
field flowers. He touched her. Her small clitoris had

shrunk in fear. Michael was patient. Slowly, gently, masterfully, he penetrated.

He closed his eyes. He remembered the years when he and Faye had made illicit love in the producer's bed. He thought of Faye's luscious golden body and gave Esther everything he had.

Esther looked at his face. It had the same ecstatic expression as when he was singing Tristan's song.

He was heavily within her, up beyond dress circle and reaching for the rafters.

He's in the wrong damn body. That's why I'm so alone. He thinks he's fucking Iseult.

A stunning finale, the roar of the crowd, and it was over. Esther was glad it was over. It had been standing room only for a long performance.

She clapped her hands.

"What's that for?"

"You were great. Like Caruso."

He smiled modestly and looked out at the sea. A man at peace. He'd dented history and made a young girl happy.

FAYE telephoned Gordon
in the afternoon. "I'm going
out tonight. Research. *The Crisis of an Aging Beauty*,
remember?"

Gordon laughed.

"Don't expect me until late."

She heard an intercom beep. That meant a long-distance call was waiting. Gordon, cheerful: "Happy sociology."

I'll sociology him, she thought, cheerlessly hanging up.

On her bed a skimpy dress, a black wig, a fox capelet bought at a thrift shop with the moths intact, a gold anklet from Woolworth's. She dressed carefully, then sat at her make-up table for cosmetic completion. From riches to rags; she spun a black web around her eyes, extended her cheekbones to her temples, rubbed a gluelike foundation around her nose and mouth, stenciled a beauty spot in a dimple, and on her curved mouth she painted a dangerous line. She was "vamp." She threw the fox around her shoulders and watched the startled doorman hail her a cab.

"Forty-seventh and Sixth," she told the driver, a balding man in his sixties who gave her an occasional intense look as he drove silently down Central Park West.

At Columbus Circle he asked shyly, "Excuse me, miss, but ain't you Pola Negri?"

She batted her eyelashes seductively and said, "Yes, I'm Miss Negri."

"Oh, my God!" cried Leon Wasserman joyously. "Wait'll I tell the missus. Pola Negri! I was crazy about you, Miss Negri. Seen every one of your pictures. I was at the funeral when you lost Mr. Valentino."

By Forty-seventh Street he was euphoric. Faye took out her purse to pay him, but he said, "Never could Leon Wasserman accept money from Pola Negri."

"You are a true fan, Mr. Wasserman." She put her hand to her mouth, kissed it, and blew it straight at him. He drove away with a hard-on. His first in many years.

Faye leaned against a grimy wall. She was unnoticed. Vamps were not a negotiable commodity on Sixth Avenue. Dracula's twilight had set. She waited patiently until a young woman with rotund thighs approached her.

"Feel like company?"

"I'm waiting for someone."

The girl regarded Faye with familiarity. "I'll wait with you."

Faye turned and walked away. The girl followed. "Don't I know you? Ain't there something about you that I know from somewhere?"

Faye was silent.

"Bad times, huh?" the girl commiserated. "Look, I can pay."

Faye turned into a bar. The girl with rotund thighs waited. Faye could see her face pressed against the window. The bar was almost empty. Faye ordered a beer and took it to a table.

A potbellied fellow with a limp joined her. "Mind company?" he asked.

"Why not?"

"Ever hear of the Spanish Civil War? I was in it. I was in the Spanish Civil War."

"I was in the movies."

"No kidding. From Hollywood!"

She nodded shyly. "Hear of Theda Bara?"

"No kidding! Theda Bara." He scratched his

stomach. "I was in the Spanish Civil War. Ever see Gary Cooper in the movie about the Spanish Civil War? I was in that war."

"Whose side were you on?"

"I don't remember. I was only there for a couple of weeks. Look, Theda. I have a terrific problem. You want to help me?"

"What is it?"

"I have a shlong. It's so long I have to strap it to my leg. I keep it strapped down like a dog. It's torture. I'll pay a hundred dollars for help."

Faye looked outside. The face was still pressed against the window. "I'm an actress. Not a nurse. Even if you were in the Spanish Civil War." She threw a dollar on the table and left.

She walked uptown with the girl with the rotund thighs beside her.

"He looked lousy. You should have come with me."

"Not interested."

"Snooty bitch. Have you heard there's a depression? Trade's not so easy nowadays."

"I'm not looking for trade."

"If it makes it easier for you to play straight, I'm game. But I can pay twenty to twenty-five dollars. Name it. It's nice with girls, gentle, affectionate. Not like with some of those rough-trade bastards."

At Fifty-third Street, Faye turned toward Fifth. She stopped in front of the Museum of Modern Art and said to her low-slung admirer, "I'm going in here. You probably are a nice girl, gentle, tender."

"And passionate," Thighs added.

But Faye pressed past her and into the museum. She flashed a membership card and went straight to the second floor, where she sank onto a banquette and eased into a world of color and line. Her own needs seemed childlike, her afternoon shabby. She asked herself why a woman who had attained comfort and stability should suddenly be searching debauch and adventure. Was this the climax of a life geared toward luxury and ease? She looked at the paintings, hoping that in this place of beauty and truth, art would supply an answer. But in fact what seemed to restore her to her comfortable low energy level was the spirit of wealth behind the room, the names of patrons in heavy gold plaques.

She rested languorously, contemplating the vicissitudes of her sudden plunge into life, when a familiar voice asked, "Can this be Faye Oppenheim playing footsie with the vice squad?"

"Don Tuttle," she said happily.

"What in hell is that costume?"

"I'm throwing myself into life," Faye said. "Into the briny deep."

"How does it feel?"

"Terrible. But then, I'm a beginner."

"The path of life is strewn with thorns," Don said ponderously. "Is this trip necessary?"

"I want to change. I've gone soft. God knows no man wants to be married to a vegetable."

Don thought of Claire and said, "If I were a

painter I'd paint you as a slut attaining redemption."

"That's pretty romantic."

"I'm in the romance business now," he said.

"At the Museum of Modern Art."

"Best place in town. Full of girls up to their ears in life or art. It's a den of repressed sensuality. So here I am, publisher of the most successful line of erotica in America. Think of what a little encouragement from an eminent guy like me means to these girls. If they could write a declarative sentence I would put them on the payroll today."

The Museum of Modern Art, a haven for soft-core pornographers, Faye thought incredulously.

"Coming in, I saw some fat dyke with her nose pressed against the window, waiting. Waiting for what? I asked myself. Is this the new hangout for the closet les? Soon as I leave I'm going to take that kid for a cup of coffee and see if she wants to do a book on Lesbos in Art."

"You may be disappointed."

"Not Don Tuttle. Living with Claire was like taking a Ph.D. in authorettes."

Faye was pensive.

"Take you, Faye—destiny brought us here today."

"Come on, Don."

"Why are you dolled up in those vampire rags? Fate! Whatever you're up to, Faye, I'll give you an advance of five hundred, sight unseen, against your first fifty pages."

Faye laughed. "I like your style, Don. It's real penny ante."

Don was suddenly business. "Promise me a first refusal and I'll give you a square legitimate deal."

Faye smiled seductively. "You'll have to deal with my agent, Gordon Oppenheim. He represents me in everything. So come and see the five o'clock movie with me and let's not talk business."

"Thanks, angel, but I've got to get home. I've got a houseful of kids waiting."

"You've remarried," Faye cried excitedly.

"Hell, no. It's my foundation, Tuttle House. Five lovelost ladies. I give them room, board and lots of encouragement. They give me—well, so far, a best seller, three paperback originals and a movie option. I've got a nun, an ex-cop, a junkie I sprung from the House of Detention. I took them off the streets, turned them on to creativeness. They think I saved them. Tuttle House. A one-man, tax-exempt foundation for saving lost souls. They get attached. Cook up a storm. Their feelings are hurt if I don't eat with them. But I'll be in touch, Faye. Remember, a first look."

Faye felt enormous affection for Don Tuttle. He'd escaped from Claire and turned all the betrayal of his own life into his own perfect tax-exempt world.

He kissed her on the cheek and skipped downstairs.

The room was quiet. A Modigliani was hanging on the wall. Its peaceful, erotic line made her feel free. She would have liked to shed her clothes and run naked through the stately rooms.

THE MUSEUM'S five o'clock movie had already started. Faye moved quietly along the darkened aisles until she found an empty seat. A Von Stroheim flickered on the screen. Faye was restive and bored. She sat for five minutes, unable to concentrate, and got up to leave.

"Mrs. Oppenheim," whispered a voice one seat over. "Is that you?"

"Who is it?"

"Karst."

"Who?"

"Esther's friend."

"I'm leaving, Karst."

"Can I come with you?"

"It's a classic."

"A boring one."

"Come along."

The two of them stepped over concentrated bodies. As Faye almost reached the aisle, she slipped and fell into a lap.

"I'm missing my film," whined a voice.

"Sorry, extremely sorry," she said, extricating herself from the large lap.

They moved toward the exit blindly and Faye sighed on reaching daylight. "It's like interrupting a religious ceremony." The two of them giggled conspiratorially.

They left the museum, walking into the late warm afternoon. Thighs was gone. Faye wondered if Don had signed her for his stable of misfits.

She put her arm through Karst's and drew him closer. He smelled the stale perfume that had soaked into her dress. It smelled cheap and raw and unclean. He felt exhilarated and pressed close to her.

Faye liked it and let him stay. She laughed. It was the way she used to laugh when she was young and aching for fame. The laugh melted away and Karst looked to see where it had gone. Her face, smudged, worn and used. Karst felt a shroud lifting.

The harness that had clamped his brain to his heart broke and he fell crazily in love.

She was a wonderful spirit that would burst like a dam and wash over him, drowning him in sin. He was small and powerless with her.

They marched along Sixth Avenue. Fresh-faced girls with flowing hair in skin-tight jeans passed by. Their innocent, thin bodies seemed contemptible to him. Karst felt linked to a woman seasoned by Babylon. God only knew to what depraved depths she would lead him. He hungered for the initiation rites into her debauched world.

He tightened his grip on her and when they arrived at Fifty-ninth and the park, Faye was bruised and sore. "I'll get a taxi here," she said.

"When can I see you?"

"You're Esther's friend."

"Yes, that's what I am, Esther's friend. Before I met Esther, I wanted to work for the *New York Times*. I thought that, and maybe a Pulitzer, must be everything a man could want. Esther turned me on to myself. She's a life-force influence, Mrs. Oppenheim. A terrific friend. But this is different. I'd always thought that man must live by his brain. Suddenly, I want to break out, to break down, to crash through. With Esther I wanted achievement. Oh, Mrs. Oppenheim, don't you understand?"

"I'm not a vamp, Karst. I'm a nice married lady."

"Oh, no, Mrs. Oppenheim, you're too vulnerable!" He took her hand and placed it on his heart. "Feel."

He placed her hand on his temple. "Feel! Oh, my God!" he cried in anguish. "Don't you understand? I'm lovesick."

He opened his mouth. She inspected. There were no gold fillings or cavities. "It's dry. Parched. I haven't any spit." He extended his arm. "Goosebumps the size of chicken pox. Don't you see, Mrs. Oppenheim, I must be in love. I have all the classic symptoms."

"It's only Tits and Ass Power. I have a repressed Tits and Ass Power factor."

"What's that?" asked Karst, bewildered.

"The dynamics are very simple. With it, you're Harlow, Monroe. Without it, you're nobody. When I was younger, I had schizophrenic Tits and Ass Power. It worked for the wrong people at the right time. My husband unexpectedly got a whiff of it. It overpowered him and he married me. Now and then it surfaces. I can't control it." She glanced at her watch. "For example, at six-thirty on the corner of Fifty-ninth and Sixth Avenue, you developed an allergy."

"Yes," he admitted. "I've caught it."

"Two aspirins and a good night's sleep. You'll be cured by tomorrow." She wiggled into a cab and waved at him through the back window.

AT SCHOOL Karst's keen and concentrated mind floated off. Moving from Latin to French Lit he began to weave a movie serial around Faye and Esther. Leaving them palpitating with fear as one class ended, he would rescue them by the next, only to dash them into a nightmare of terror as the bell rang for study.

Karst pitted mother against daughter. He was a dybbuk, a spirit that possessed them both, and as the day passed, he created a reign of terror for the two victims. By three o'clock he was exhausted. He felt as if he had spent the whole day masturbating.

He wandered the halls into the offices of the *Open Harte*. The disorder, the kidding around between Zimmerman and the girls, this had always seemed to him foreplay for the big time. But today it seemed drab. He sat down to write his editorial, but visions of Faye floated naked before him. He suddenly knew he must have her. He threw aside his editorial and opened a fresh notebook.

USED-UP WOMAN
by R. Karst

FAYE climbed into bed that night and clung close to Gordon.

"Feeling neglected, honey?"

"Little."

He pulled her close. "I know. Things are so damn active now."

She stroked his stomach, ran her hand across his chest. He closed his eyes and let her touch lull him. The day was over; the ferment, the fever, the placating and soothing now dim.

"Do you love me?" she asked.

"Yes," he said, "I love you."

They lay there, overlapping one another in silence.

"Working?" he finally said.

"Puttering."

His eyes were closed. "Michael Stone's in the hospital. Abdominal obstruction. Poor guy's in terrible pain."

"You're so busy, Gordon. I'll go over to see him tomorrow."

"It'll cheer him, poor bastard. They're running every test on him. Hope he's okay. He's almost finished with his novel and we have a deal with Warner's for a first look."

Faye leaned back on her pillows. She had just seen Mike and Claire Tuttle lunching at the Oak Room. Had they made love that afternoon? Making love to Claire could create a toxic reaction, she thought. Poor Annabelle. What a threadbare existence to be married to a professional Don Juan. Annabelle, submerging her pain into dark and violent poetry. Michael's philandering grossing them a penthouse on Fifth Avenue and a weekend place in Connecticut.

Gordon was a philanderer too, Faye realized. All his sexual energies went into contracts and deals, and she was left with the residue of a heavy day at the office. She felt a sudden kinship to Annabelle. She would call her tomorrow after she had seen Mike.

DOCTORS Hospital stood adjacent to the East River. It overlooked the mayor's house and garden.

The hospital corridor had a dignified calm. One did not feel confronted with his own mortality as he entered the austere foyer. It felt rather like visiting a friend who was taking a rest. Surgery, pain and death were restricted, like mad dogs, to the upper floors.

Faye took the elevator to the seventh floor and walked along the black linoleum floors to 7008. She cautiously opened the door. "How are you feeling?" she asked the suffering novelist.

"That goddamn bitch! Cunt!"

Faye thought he was hallucinating. She sat beside him.

"I've just gotten the results," he said. "Arsenic. That bitch has been poisoning me."

"What's happened?" Faye asked excitedly.

"Annabelle! She's slowly killing me. It was bad enough having her goddamn long-suffering soul hang over the house like a shroud. But then she started putting cockroach powder into my morning cornflakes. A dose of arsenic for dear old Michael and off to her fucking poems."

"Poor Michael," said Faye, barely able to contain her delight.

"Annabelle and her goddamn poetry. She's a god-damn arsenicist. She said she couldn't take any more of my playing around, that all she wanted was to disable me. I'll show that cunt what it takes to disable Michael Stone."

He reached for Faye and dragged her toward him. He kissed her heavily, intensely. He drew her to him with the power of a wave being sucked back into the sea. Their love seemed enchanted, timeless. Sweet as *Seventh Heaven.* Faye felt soft and vulnerable.

Michael Stone was still a moment of ecstasy in a life of sexual accommodation. She wanted him desperately.

The arsenic victim had a pneumatic erection and

Faye tumbled toward it blindly and sucked it deep into her larynx.

"I love you!" she gargled.

"Annabelle's told my lawyer it was a crime of passion. He says I shouldn't prosecute. That shyster!"

He looked down at her thoughtfully. "You're still a hot blonde, Faye. You're still my Mary Magdalene."

Faye glided up from down. She felt a flush of self-disgust.

"You smelled so blond," he reminisced.

"Was that all?" she asked. "Just blond?"

"You were so golden. So gentile. It was like fucking the New Testament."

Shikse pussy? Was that it? Grinding out some biblical fantasy for a hungry Jew from New York? She thought it had been real. Product: a Malibu bed, a Gideon Bible, a blond body. It had been like that even when she thought it wasn't. Aching, she wondered if she had clung to her bed like a nun all these years to avoid that reality. To atone to Gordon.

"I'm not Mary Magdalene any more," she said. "I'm your agent's wife."

"You may be my agent's wife in his bed, but in mine you'll always be a blond angel." His heart pumped generously as he bestowed immortality upon Faye. "I'm glad Gordon gets my ten percent. You deserve every nickel."

She closed the door behind her and passed a nurse walking toward his room.

Michael had opened an old scar. She could smell

the blood. She thought of his disabled body and his raging erection. Hell, if arsenic doesn't wither it, the human race may survive after all, she decided with New Testament compassion, and she forgave both him and herself.

WHEN ESTHER met
Karst, something dropped
out of her life. The source of energy transporting her
into the crotch of fame and fortune dried up. She felt
her specialness, her enchanted puberty, turn into a
heavy weight. She gave up Mick Jagger and Janis
Joplin, and flung herself into Bach Cantatas. She
sensed her youth passing by as if she were an on-
looker at a parade, and she sobbed wistfully over her
lost ambition to fuck famous men. She had been

weaned on them. They had always been in her house.
As a baby they had dangled her, held her on their
knees and told her stories; and then, as she glided into
adolescence, they had entered her and that had made
her special. Sitting between a Pulitzer Prize novelist
and a National Book Award poet on her mother's
velvet couch was a security blanket which she had
carried with her from birth.

And suddenly she didn't care. She had let go. She
had fallen in love with the immigrant son of Polish
exiles, a shy, square boy who had listened to her and
then cut her off. Karst did not call her. He was pleasant to her in the halls, but he wandered off toward
some secret Karst world. Esther was lovesick. Was this
the way great literary courtesans behaved? Would
Madame de Staël have grieved over a Polish virgin?
Never! In her perplexed state she cried over the death
of a great ambition.

FAYE was now adjusted to the fact that life wasn't there. She had to go out and create it.

She thought cheerlessly of the Spanish Civil War victim with the endless shlong. Must I submit to that to know experience? Surely writers didn't go out each day tracking down peculiarity and aberration in order to write. She couldn't imagine Claire Tuttle or Michael Stone or Paul Samuels slavishly degrading themselves for each new chapter. What were the alternative ways to find material? Where and how, she sat pondering.

The possibilities. She made a list and graded each on a scale of one to five:

1. Karst. An affair with her daughter's friend. Familiar movie theme, *The Graduate*. Disadvantages: Faye's guilt toward Esther.   ONE

2. Paul Samuels. He was heavy into revisions and had gone into seclusion. Hadn't called in two weeks. Threesome with Paul and Laura had possibilities, though Gordon had said recently that the market on threesomes was down. However, a West Side *partouze*, urban, chic, a sure paperback sale. Paul's revisions had priority. She must wait on this.   TWO

3. Michael Stone. Profligate husband of stoic, long-suffering Annabelle whose pain appeared quarterly in the pages of *Partisan Review*. Annabelle's swift revenge.   THREE

4. Claire Tuttle. A lesbian novel. Claire, nubile and cool. Ready for anything. Disadvantages: Claire's facility and speed. An affair with Claire would be out in hardback under Claire's name in six months. Claire was out. She'd beat Faye to a draw with the same material, a bigger advance and a larger sale. Too humiliating.   ZERO

5. Ulu Ubango. Much research on New Zealand eliminated a long piece on Ubango. Besides,

he was probably into a novel on America and she would surely be in it somewhere.   ONE-HALF

6. Don Tuttle. Don's change of life. Easygoing cuckolded husband transformed into hustling publisher. Don, patriarch to a commune of misfits. *There was her story.* In Don's household she would find a life force far removed from her airless and insular world. She could not be accused of stealing her daughter's lover, her husband's client or a family friend. Here right off the streets like a pushcart. COME!!! It stretched out its hand toward her. Don Tuttle, evangelist to life's social outcasts, preparing these orphans of the storm for a life of subsidiary rights, reprint sales and the possibility of a one-way trip to Hollywood.   FIVE

KARST had to see Faye. He called her and she laughed at him and he felt like an orphan. He decided to wait outside her apartment and abduct her into a waiting cab.

He hung around the Oppenheim apartment building afternoons and evenings, but Faye did not emerge. Karst called her again.

"I'm extremely busy," she said. "I'm not leaving the house. If you want to peel your banana, come on up and peel it here."

His problem was to avoid Esther, so he cut classes and arrived at the apartment at eleven o'clock. He wore suede trousers and an imported Italian shirt. He felt like Jean-Paul Belmondo.

"You're recovered," she said.

"God, no. I'm in agony."

"Epsom Salts and hot baths soften and heal," she said.

"You must help me."

"No. It's not my problem."

The bitch clearly didn't give a damn about his gonads. "Take a scholar and create a sexual Frankenstein and it's your problem," he said.

"You're my daughter's friend and I don't believe in incest."

"I'm a virgin," he cried. "How can it be incest if I'm a virgin?"

Faye thought about a chapter on a virgin who fancied himself a Don Juan. "Come with me," she said and went into the bedroom. "I can't go to bed with you," she said. "But I can show you some tricks."

"What do I do?"

"Try instinct," she said and pulled down silk pants.

There it was, a tangled brush of hair, the key to sexual freedom. He ran his fingers through it.

"A kiss," she said. "Your first lesson."

"Oh, God, no," he said. "I can't do that."

"Class is over," she said and pulled up her pants.

"All right, all right. I'll do it."

She pulled them down again and Karst sucked in enough air to take him under water for three minutes.

It felt like Equatorial Africa. Her heat, her sourish taste and wiry hair repelled him. He wanted to vomit. He felt like the dying hero in *The Snows of Kilimanjaro*. He needed quinine and a doctor.

Faye pushed him away. "You're cured," she said. "Go back to Emerson and Thoreau."

"I can't," he said. "I'm in too deep."

"Get a whore."

"They seem so cold and sad."

There was no material in this petulant virgin and Faye wanted him out of her house. "You're not ready for fun and games," she said.

"If you don't mind my getting fresh, Mrs. Oppenheim, you're a prick-tease."

She laughed. "It's my repressed Tits and Ass Power. I warned you."

But Karst's lovesick balls had undergone a mutation. His longing had turned to fury. He felt mortified that he had disclosed himself to this woman. He had debased himself. He rushed from her room, from her house into the open. The park, glittering in the sun, only ripened his humiliation. He felt like an open wound. He wanted to hurt her. He walked home slowly, thinking about Faye, thinking about his book, *Used-Up Woman*.

Thoughts of that cheap slut and what he would do to her fanned his rage into ecstasy. Wait until

Used-Up Woman hit the bookstores. What revenge!
He'd show that bitch—and he'd use her husband as
his agent.

FAYE fudged and kept procrastinating and finally called Don Tuttle.

"Tuttle House," purred a fake English voice.

"Will you tell Mr. Tuttle that Mrs. Oppenheim is calling, please."

"One min-nut, please."

Faye was put on hold and then Don burst on. "I've been waiting. Where've you been?"

"It's not about a book, Don. I need a favor. Can I join your household?"

"Love it," Don said. "My first rich outcast. My last girls were a bumper crop. There's a new bunch now."

"Don, you're a lifesaver."

"I'll call the girls and have them fix a place. Just fill out the forms."

"But I thought it was just an informal group."

"Honey, I'm a creative foundation. The tax guys are breathing down my neck. With two books on the best-seller list I had to incorporate. See you at dinner. Glad you're on board."

Faye telephoned Gordon. "Darling, I think I've got something but I can't concentrate here. Can you and Esther manage if I go to the Hamptons for a week?"

"Atta girl. We'll be fine. Just come back with fifty pages and you can buy five acres of your own."

Faye packed her bag, left a note for Esther and took a taxi crosstown.

FAYE arrived at a Victorian brownstone on East Eighty-second Street. A massive oak door held a brass plate with the inscription TUTTLE HOUSE. A wail of chords from an ailing piano rolled through the walls. Faye rang the bell and the piano gurgled and died. Faye heard footsteps and the sliding of many locks.

The door opened and the girl with the rotund thighs said, "Hello, Mrs. Oppenheim. I don't know if you remember me. I'm Clarissa Lowenthal. We met on Sixth Avenue." She picked up Faye's bag. "I'm in the middle of practicing, so I can't give you the grand tour."

"Are you doing *Lesbos in Art* for Don?"

"Don was putting you on. We met at a concert over a year ago and afterward we went out for a drink. He gave me an advance against my novel, *The Violent Violinist*. Did you read it?"

"No."

"I gave my first recital with the money. I'm hoping with my new book I'll be able to afford Town Hall."

"You're a musician?"

"A concert pianist. But classical music is a lousy way to make a living, so I write novels to subsidize my career."

"Why not teach?" Faye asked.

"Teach kiddies at eight dollars an hour? I have a three-thousand-dollar advance on my next book. Do you know how many kids I'd have to teach to make that?"

Faye smiled.

"I'm wild about this one. My heroine is a lesbian concert pianist who finds artistic inspiration by plunging into the lower depths of society."

"A musical Dorian Gray."

"That's it," said Clarissa. "I saw you and you seemed a natural. When Don came out of the museum and told me who you were, I didn't take your rejection so personally."

Faye followed Clarissa up a carved mahogany

stairway into a small room. It contained a sagging army cot, a small wooden table and an unpainted chest of drawers. There were no shades on the window.

"Cozy as a prison cell," Faye said.

"Don's a spartan. He says comfort distracts an artist. He says writers that get too comfortable go soft."

"What about curtains? I can't get up at six o'clock."

"Don wants us up by natural light. He says when you're half asleep you can slip into your book before you've had a chance to get blocked. He was married to Claire Tuttle, you know, and he knows a lot of writer's tricks."

Faye decided this was Don's revenge on women writers. "Sounds like the army," she said.

"You can't imagine the nuts we've had, Mrs. Oppenheim. Don had to tighten up."

"You don't seem to mind this frugal atmosphere."

"When a guy gives me a chance to launch a concert career, I'm goddamn grateful. He can run Tuttle House like Sing Sing as long as I've got Brahms. Anyhow, this is hustle time. See you at dinner."

She closed the door and Faye surveyed the small, grim room. She lay on the cot, which sank beneath her as knots of stuffing surfaced. She thought of her downy bed at home and she cursed Gordon for chasing her out into the world to find a new meaning to her life.

She lay on the bed watching the shifting sun. Slowly, she built her case against Gordon. She placed one piece of evidence against another like a tightening noose. By the time the sun had drifted over the Hudson and the room was a rosy glow, she'd constructed an airtight case against Gordon Oppenheim which any jury in America would support.

THE jury had returned with its verdict. The foreman stood and announced: "Gordon Oppenheim guilty in the second degree of premeditated intent to drive the defendant insane. The jury recommends Gordon Oppenheim be confined to fifty years of solitude on the thirty-third floor of his Sixth Avenue office."

A knock aroused Faye from her reverie. "Who is it?"

"Annabelle Stone."

Faye opened the door and the two women embraced.

"Come into the cell."

Annabelle entered the dingy room and sat on the pockmarked bed.

"How's the food?" Faye asked.

"Terrible. Don's stingy, mean and miserly. A greedy huckster, and Claire's entitled to every dime she ever made off him."

"But you're glowing, radiant," Faye said.

"Revenge. Such a satisfying emotion. I'm finally even with that bastard and I'll be rich and famous to boot. No more obscure little poetess, believe me."

"But, Annabelle . . ."

"The moment they diagnosed arsenic I called Don Tuttle. Less than ten minutes after my call he was over with a book contract. He thinks there may be something in it for Jane Fonda."

"Annabelle, you must feel something besides euphoria. I mean, you did try to kill your husband."

"Faye, how can you think that? I only wanted to disable him."

"With arsenic?"

"Try to understand how it feels to wake up each morning of your life to the fact that somewhere, somehow, your husband will make love to another woman. Smudged lipstick, hairpins, the most banal evidence. Good friends commiserating. And worst of all, having to read about his insidious prick in each of his books.

Watching Michael's prick make the best-seller list year after year was killing me. I was at my wit's end."

"So you poisoned him."

"For God's sake, I merely put his lousy prick out of commission. Michael works at night. Then he goes into the kitchen for a snack. Well, in New York there's always a stray cockroach. He'd scream and yell and accuse me of being a lousy housewife, and if I really loved him there'd be no roaches when he went for his snack. I used to lie in bed and wonder why he wasn't fucking me instead of carrying on about some lousy cockroach. But no, Michael couldn't waste his precious sperm in his wife when he could be humping some idiot the following day. The best-seller list is a shrine in our house. Michael kisses it three times at sunset. Anyhow, one night he came to bed without even a hello and began screaming about some roach. I decided ENOUGH. Michael begins his day with a morning ritual of reading the obituaries as he eats his cornflakes and black coffee. I decided to flick some roach powder into the cereal. I thought he might suffer a mild discomfort, acid indigestion. He wouldn't feel like fucking—it worked. All the usual telltale signs of betrayal disappeared. No hairpins, no obscene red smudges. Michael developed a lassitude. He stayed at home. He began to write themes other than swashbuckling fuckers. His last book was a suspense thriller. It didn't make the best-seller list, but it did well in paperback. He became childlike, dependent. He stopped screaming about cockroaches because he

was in bed with me. Our marriage became affectionate. Then one morning I got careless. The phone rang
and I accidentally gave him too much. Michael developed a violent stomach ache and his doctor ordered
him to the hospital. That's when they discovered the
arsenic.

"I thought of myself as a desperate wife. I was
invisible, long-suffering. Michael had the fame, the
awards. I had an audience of twenty-five people who
read the *Peoria Review*.

"Barely a week passed and I was a celebrity. Interviews with the BBC, an invitation from Carson; I
even got an offer for a daytime program of my own
called 'Disenfranchised Woman.' All those years of
pain, of enduring Michael's endless infidelities, no one
looked my way. Now that I'm the Cockroach Arsenicist, men are flocking. I always thought it was women
who were masochists, but it's not so. Men are just as
eager for punishment."

A knock interrupted their talk.

"Who's there?" asked Annabelle.

"Lois."

"Lois Pulanski. Don't say anything while she's
here."

Lois Pulanski was a leggy blonde with a long,
lean back. She seemed frisky as a drum majorette.
"Hello there," she said. "How about a Scotch to get
acquainted? How far along are you?"

"Into what?"

"Your book. How far into your book? What'd you
say the subject was?"

"I didn't say."

"Discretion," said Annabelle. "You must be discreet about Faye. She could close Tuttle House down."

"Hey, you're not CIA?" said Lois excitedly. "You've got classified government papers, right?"

Faye smiled discreetly.

"I almost balled a President," Lois said. "But there was a national emergency and he broke the date. He never called back."

"Lousy luck."

"You bet. I got so damn mad I decided to fuck his Cabinet. Secretary of State, Secretary of Labor, Secretary of Defense. I was halfway through the Cabinet and into his Harvard consultants. I was going like wildfire when elections came up and the Democrats got voted out."

"Pity."

"Not really. By then I was into the academics. Harvard led to Yale, Yale to Princeton. It was a perpetual education. I had worked my way through the Ivy League and into the Midwest when elections rolled around again and I found myself back in office."

"So you've finally made it with the President?"

"Not yet. But I've got a date with his speech writer next week, and if the goddam Russians and Chinese and Indians can control themselves, I figure the President is two weeks off."

DINNER consisted of a stringy roast swaddled in pork fat, green, saltless beans, wilted salad and Romeo Salta wine. The ladies chewed at the pitiful animal, wondering if it was worth the slaughter. But Lois was skimming along into the great old days, doggedly fucking the Directors Guild and Screenwriters West. She crossed state lines, surfaced for breath and surrendered to shady casino landlords.

Don smiled happily at his virtuoso, his golden

girl. He figured that by Lois's own calculations, she had fucked over six hundred men in the over-seventy-five-percent tax bracket. She was a pioneer, traveling by convertible Mercedes instead of covered wagon over the prairies and into the heartland of America. She had invaded America like a tank, feasting on bodies of movie stars, cattle kings, robber barons, publishers, the Congress and the President's Cabinet. Her capacities were unlimited and her memory pitch-perfect. She retained every detail.

Yet, Don worried. When he first discovered her (in his own bed yet), he knew instinctively that through Lois Pulanski he could reach the real America, out beyond the Jersey Turnpike. Lois was his open sesame into the homes of millions of housewives whose lives centered around *TV Guide*. He put her to work and she proved apt and eager. Her semiliterate confessions flooded supermarkets and ten-cent stores. *Afternoons in a Hollywood Motel, A Night on the Senate Floor, Snow White and the Seven Diamonds,* were gobbled up like Tootsie Rolls. Lois was happy seeing her name on the sleazy covers that bombarded America. Don called her his little Scheherazade and gave her a three-thousand-dollar advance on each of her thousand-and-one-nights.

Then Lois came upon Colette. She was enchanted by that great lady's amours. She asked Don to buy her Jane Austen. She grew ashamed of her name on those lurid paperback covers.

"But pulp is as American as apple pie," Don said.

"You're reviving a lost American art form."

"I no longer feel creative in pulp," she said.

She insisted on taking creative-writing courses; she wanted to join the PEN club, to bed and eventually marry a Pulitzer novelist. In lust lies knowledge.

Don realized the handicap. A creative-writing course would destroy her semiliterate trademark. He realized that if she got into the hands of the boys at Elaine's bar, his goose was cooked.

And Lois was afraid. She was running through her repertoire fast. She thought a change might mean a new market, a new career. She felt that if she could hit the Harold Robbins audience, join Jacqueline Susann on the talk shows, she would emerge from her sordid pulp profile.

Her change was swift. She began diverting the others from their work. She lingered in their cubicles pretending friendship, asking questions, but one day Annabelle walked into her room and saw Lois scavaging her notes. Annabelle kicked her out, had a lock installed and boycotted her.

Lois tried a tryst with Clarisse. But when Clarisse was not researching degeneracy, she was at the piano with her beloved Brahms, dreaming of her Town Hall debut.

To gain Faye's confidence, Lois revealed sections of her new book. Faye seemed uninterested.

Don felt increasingly nervous about Lois. He had launched a new generation of pulp writers. The Tuttle House imprint was responsible for resuscitating a dying art form. He investigated the possibility of buying the copyright name, Lois Pulanski, but he discovered that if Lois left Tuttle House her name went along with her.

Then he ran into Lois lunching with a rival publisher at the Italian Pavilion and he knew her days with him were numbered. He smiled at her and seemed unperturbed. He'd gotten her finest nights. Soon Lois would peak.

Both Don and Lois realized these were her last days at Tuttle House. She had decided to go with the rival publisher and Don was on to a new angle. He would create a name, copyright it, and then writers could come or go, it didn't matter. Anyone could write the stories, he owned the name. His eye was on Faye Cassidy.

It was a cheery night. Don blinked sentimentally and toasted Lois: "From Tuttle House to America, the Golden Girl of Celebrity Fucking."

She smiled affectionately at her mentor. Without him, she might have married a rich old man and declined into a life of bridge and diamonds. Now, a wordsmith, she'd have the diamonds and to hell with the old man. She yearned for the big strike; the sale to the movies; the heavy bidding by the reprint houses; her endorsement of other books appearing in the *New York Times* book ads. But she was frightened. Her vein might go dry before she'd hit pay dirt. It was time to leave.

Her voice, low and luscious, murmured, "To Don Tuttle, who championed my creative journey into the world of *l'amour*."

"I may vomit," Annabelle whispered to Faye.

"I wonder how it feels to screw ten guys a day?"

Annabelle shivered. She saw Lois as Michael's counterpart. She saw them together, tearing away at the other's private parts as they planned their following day's work.

"Five, ten, fifty. What's the difference? The only way she'll hit the lists is by tits and testicles."

"She's breaking with her past. Says her new one's about homicide."

"Who told you?" Annabelle asked concernedly.

"She did. *Irish Coffee Murder*. Cute title."

"What else did she say?"

"Hmmm . . . something about a wife who murders her famous husband. He's a cold remote bastard, never touches her, only works. Well, in going through his papers she discovers he was a homosexual."

Faye began to dawdle as she noticed Lois stiffen.

"Uh, she decides to revenge herself by publishing his memoirs, posthumously. She becomes famous—"

"Plagiarism!" Annabelle screamed. "That bitch has plagiarized my novel. Instead of cornflakes, she's substituted Irish whiskey. But it's mine, *The Cornflakes Murder Mystery*."

"Castrator!" Lois roared. "I didn't plagiarize anything."

"Careful," Annabelle warned. "I don't take that from sluts."

"I'll slut you, you strychnine sadist!" Lois walked firmly toward her, and raising both her arms, lowered them about Annabelle's waist in a body hold taught her by an ex-Marine sergeant. The two women grappled and tumbled about and Annabelle sank to the floor as Lois, returning to the law of the jungle, sank two capped teeth into her lip. A wail of pain.

"Animals! Is this the thanks Tuttle gets? After everything I've done for you bitches!"

Blood flowed from Annabelle's open lip. "Call a goddamn plumber," Lois said triumphantly. "Your faucet's leaking."

Annabelle raised herself, reached for a plate and hurled it at her tormentor. But in her weakened condition she miscalculated and the plate smashed into Clarisse, covering her with congealed brown gravy.

"My concert dress!" she screamed and rushed toward the exhausted poetess. She placed her fat fingers around Annabelle's neck and Annabelle saw the end. She said a last rite for herself (iambic pentameter), she forgave Michael and hoped that he would cry at her funeral.

Lois threw herself between the two impacted women. "Forgive me, Annabelle," she cried guiltily. "I only wanted to write about murder. My book has nothing to do with homosexual husbands. I'm so goddamn bored with orgasms," she sobbed. "Eroticism revolts me. He's the enemy. A tax-exempt pimp." She pointed a finger at Don. "*J'accuse! J'accuse!* Bastard! It's you who gets rich off our misery and pain. You . . . sexual Fagin." She viewed her glorious exploited body with tears in her eyes.

Faye gazed in disbelief at the screaming, disheveled women.

Don remembered Claire. If he had survived marriage to that bloodsucker, he would survive the Tuttle House uprising. Pulling himself together, he was once again paternal Papa Don. "Girls, I have nothing to offer you but blood, toil, sweat and tears—"

"Bullshit!"

That was it! The final injustice! "You think I run a creative center on peanuts. All you ingrates supply is product. I, Don Tuttle, publisher, take it, package it, promote it and feed it to the American housewife where she lives. What Mrs. U.S.A. doesn't get from her husband she gets from me. That's where the goddamn money goes." He sensed a calm and went for the jugular. "All writers get blocked. Even the big boys. It's part of the business. So do we turn this place into an insane asylum or keep it a haven for young talent?"

The girls were silent.

"Sleep on it."

The girls trudged upstairs and into their rooms. Faye heard the clicking of locks. She placed a chair beneath her doorknob. Fledgling authors barely able to fly, already dreaming of the great migration onto the *New York Times* best-seller list. Each little writer protecting her small fund of experience from the scavengers. Tuttle House, a tax shelter of suspicion and chaos.

The house was quiet. Yet Faye could feel the hostile breath of her colleagues as they plotted themselves to sleep.

Her room was dark. Faye got up, packed her bag and tiptoed from the house. She flagged a cab and went home.

ESTHER's listlessness
went unnoticed. Gordon
was manipulating contracts and geniuses and Faye
was fluttering toward life like a savage moth.

Esther was discouraged. Her father's client list
oppressed her. She no longer yearned to grab fame by
its balls. She fell into a lassitude and thought only
of Karst.

She read a French folk tale in which a vengeful
husband punished his wife by cementing her within

the walls of their castle. The fate of the sealed and cemented woman haunted her. She felt her obsession for Karst was sealing *her* off from life. She must free herself.

She waited until Friday and then went to his office. Karst's head was bowed in prayer but his hand scribbled mercilessly. He looked like Moses engraving upon the tablets.

"I miss you, Karst."

"Go away. I'm working." He didn't look up.

A nip of pain, strong as prime Polish vodka, convulsed her. "When can I see you?"

He looked at her without seeing her. "You're disturbing me."

Her heart split into infinite fragments, each jagged one ripping her in grief. It was like Bach, pure and sublime. She wanted to cry. The Pulitzer Prize author and the National Book Award winner had not roused her to such torment and they had both fucked her. It was Karst, a virgin Pole, who reached her. Lovesick, she looked at him with eyes heavy as an oil slick.

She filled him with contempt. Her slavish mien was corpselike. He yearned to place her in a coffin and lower her slowly into the ground.

Guilt draped itself around his balls. He felt trapped in the carnage. It was a heady excitement, a breakthrough. He stumbled back to *Used-Up Woman*, scribbling with renewed insight.

Esther was wild with grief. She was humiliated,

degraded. She walked away from Karst newborn, a victim. Her misery swept her across the park and into her room.

"Oh God, love is hell!" she moaned, and she wept sweet and grievous tears.

BEFORE Gordon was awake, Faye was already at work. He breakfasted on his usual croissant and espresso and listened happily to Faye plucking at her Olivetti. It had a lyrical sound, a throb, a pulse. Gordon felt as though music were filling his home. There was a new sense of life this morning and Gordon had visions of Faye growing into her prime, spinning merry little tales of love.

The days lengthened into weeks and Gordon

came and went. Faye was constant, her fingers dexterous. She stuck to the saddle, taking meals in her room, nodding detachedly to her husband as he passed in and out of bed.

Esther occasionally passed through the room. She kissed her diligent mother and scanned a few pages as if she were witnessing a miracle.

Faye was embarked on a typing marathon. Papers accumulated in growing piles on her night table. She was like an invalid, scarcely leaving her room, existing on tea, toast and broiled meats. Gordon passed his evenings in his study.

On the sixty-fourth night of her seclusion, Faye put her manuscript in order and read it through for the first time. She felt flushed, dissatisfied. It lacked something. She thought about the last months. All the fucking was the same, detached, manipulated.

She sank back into the cozy warmth of her pillows and thought about her marriage. Brief kisses goodnight; loneliness despite his body beside hers; fits and seizures of small despair; magic and dream found at the movies.

She had married him to escape careless nights, sexual humiliations, feeling like leftover scraps. She'd married Gordon to cut her losses. Suddenly she didn't want a blue-chip stock. She wanted a lover, a husband. She thought of her industrious Gordon sitting downstairs, and she yearned to share her dream with him and enter once again into his.

"Gordon!" she cried.

He bounced from his chair and rushed upstairs toward her urgent and animated cry.

Faye sat under the flowered coverlet, her manuscript by her side.

She'd done it! She'd come through! Gordon went toward the manuscript, magnetized. Dollar signs were in his eyes. Faye felt like a hot property.

"No, darling, here, to me."

"What are you doing?"

She reached for him, wrapped her arms around him, stroked and warmed him.

She had the smell of a Hollywood premiere. He pressed close, clumsily, hungrily, and stiffened as he entered her.

She tried to enter and share with him the enchanted world of *Seventh Heaven*. But the years of subversive fantasy which had kept them apart separated them now. The doors were closed. Gordon entered alone, leaving Faye outside waiting.

I will never be *Diane* and Gordon will never be *Chico*. That's how it is. That's what will be. She seemed to watch some mythical figures fly off into the sky.

She looked at Gordon and love, a small dream, a lingering adolescence, blazed brightly as a Los Angeles brush fire, and then burned low, in some distant funeral pyre inside her: mortal now, flickering.

Life is not a silent movie, she thought. It has sound. Life is not technicolor. It is mottled and gray. There is no sound track. There are no comfortable dissolves or wipes. Life, shot for shot, is not Boffo, does not make it in the hinterlands, or, for that matter, on Central Park West.

Life is, simply, Gordon and Faye. She turned toward him and said, "Touch me." He put his hand on hers. She was peaceful. She held his hand and she felt survival, a small, imperfect, but satisfying victory.

GORDON looked at her—
his Faye—with pride. He
viewed the manuscript pages surrounding them as a
new romance.

"Let me have it," he said.

"Still needs work."

"Let me be the judge." He reached out to take
it.

"It's not in order. Wait downstairs and I'll bring
it to you."

"All right," he said and went downstairs.

Faye scanned it anxiously. Then she took it down to him. "It's done . . . I think." She handed it to him.

Gordon lurched into profound affability as if he were told that his wife had just delivered a seven-pound son. "Congratulations, darling. I knew you could do it."

"I want to publish it under a pseudonym."

"You're a silly, foolish girl. You're entering your postpartum depression, Faye. Writing a book is no different than having a baby."

"Is that what I'm having?"

"Of course, my angel. All writers are alike. You've been working like a son of a bitch and now comes the moment of judgment. I'm damn proud of you, Faye. Now get out of here and let me read."

Faye sat far above the city in her room on a satin chaise while Gordon, one floor below, sat in his soft leather chair reading her book. Looking out of her tower, she felt like a princess. Outside the limestone walls lay the small, fierce kingdom in which she and Gordon lived so lavishly. Gordon was her feudal knight who went forth daily to joust with the foes and return to her at night with a bag of gold.

And here in her tower, she passed the life of a bored chattel, lazy, lengthy days warding off depressions with naps; suppressing desire by extensive phone calls; and in tunics of expensive matte jersey, awaiting the good provider's return. It was a life of anesthetized dreams and repressed ambition.

Faye wondered if she had jeopardized her privileged position. Suppose Gordon liked her book. Would he insist she follow it with another? Suppose Gordon hated it. Would she sink into disgrace if he couldn't sell it? Was it worth the frantic fucking and sucking to appease a husband who felt that his wife should be doing something creative with her life?

A far simpler solution: volunteer at a hospital for foundlings. Any indifferent meritorious work which might consume some hours and satisfy Gordon.

She sat pondering her fate when Gordon rushed in, his face livid, his eyes dead and cold. "How could you do this to me? Your husband! Your mate!"

"Gordon, what have I done?"

"I trusted you. I believed in you. I urged you to do something with your life."

"What's upsetting you so, Gordon?"

"Oh, my God," he moaned. "Is this the thanks I get?" Gordon was pacing back and forth, wringing his hands, his head bowed as in prayer.

"For Christ's sake, Gordon. What's the matter?"

"A book! You call this a book? Such betrayal! A tribute to Judas!"

"Gordon, you're imagining—"

"You slept with my friends. You slept with my clients. My Pulitzer Prize winner you went down on. And you call it a book!"

"Gordon, you're mad."

Gordon started screaming, "I'm not halfway through, but I recognize pulp autobiography. Here, page four. I dare you to tell me that Peter Sargent isn't Paul Samuels. You didn't even have the courtesy to finish Chapter One before you were fucking my Pulitzer Prize author." This seemed the greatest blow to Gordon, the hallowed Pulitzer between his wife's loins.

"All I can say is that you are crazy, Gordon, stark crazy."

"Crazy? Deny that Ulu Ubango isn't Arthur Turoonu."

"For God's sake, Gordon, do you honestly think that a man destined for a Nobel Prize would stick his nose up his agent's wife's clitoris? Come on, be reasonable."

"Jesus, Faye, that you could be this reckless."

"I swear. You're imagining things. Finish the book. You'll see how foolish you are."

"Faye, I am warning you. I am warning you from the depths of my soul. If I find that there's one word of truth in this . . ."

"I swear, Gordon, on my mother's hallowed name."

"I hope you're not lying, Faye. For your sake."

And Gordon was out the door.

Faye sat waiting. She no longer felt the princess. Her tiara was paste, her kingdom shaky, her security jeopardized. Why hadn't she let things alone? Why hadn't she resisted Gordon? He would have nagged her for a while, and then, sensing her indifference, would have left her alone. What a fool she'd been. She could have slept out her days in luxury and peace if only she'd stayed passive. She should have kept her own counsel, followed her own heart. She was a perfect concubine: pleasant, elegant, bending to Gordon's will. Instead she'd fallen into his trap, the self-achievement trap, and the consequences seemed disastrous. She'd been sure that he'd be amused, treating it as just another little schlock novel with the chance of a paperback sale. The whole thing was a drastic mistake. She looked out of her window, her world in crisis, her dreams collapsed.

Slowly she began to realize that self-pity is tantamount to confession. And so she began to build a line of defense that every agent must believe.

In another half-hour Gordon returned, the manuscript in his hand.

"You *are* fast," she said, complimenting him.

"I'm still not finished—but I recognize my wife's lies. Here, page forty-nine, I dare you to deny that that is Michael Stone. How could you do that with a man recuperating from arsenic poisoning?"

Faye looked shocked. "Gordon," she said with great dignity, "you are supposed to be a great agent. You understand a writer's mind. You know a writer will find a detail, disguise it, use it as a foundation for something else. Yes, you know all about writers. Yet, you automatically assume that anything I write must be autobiographical. You have no respect for me, Gordon. You think I'm a nothing. A housewife. An object. A beautiful body with a dumb befuddled brain, incapable of anything more challenging than boiling an egg."

"That's not so, Faye. I have great respect for you. You're my wife."

"Does Claire Tuttle undergo this inquisition every time she turns in a book?"

Gordon fidgeted. "Promise me again that nothing in this book is true. Swear it!"

"Don't ask me for any goddamn promises, Gordon. Get Hemingway to promise! Get Mailer to promise! Get Proust to promise!"

Defeated, Gordon took the manuscript and left.

Faye decided the hell with it and went to bed. She was almost asleep when Gordon came in. He turned on the light and sat by her side. "Faye," he said, "I believe you. There's something in it, something strange, but I believe you."

She saw a change in his face. Like the subtle loss of soul that occurs when a face is replaced by a photograph.

"I'll call Random House tomorrow. This is their sort of thing. Columbia is desperate for something for Ali McGraw. This may be it."

Something died in his eyes. Something new replaced it. The warmth left his hands. His voice became honey. She felt like a client.

He believes in it, she said to herself. He thinks I'm a writer.

Gordon looked at her with agent's eyes. "We'll make a fortune," he said.

They smiled at each other, neither knowing what about.

THE *following fall a*
widely traveled manuscript,
Used-Up Woman, *was hanging around. Don Tuttle*
picked it up for fifteen hundred dollars and published
it as a paperback original.

Number nine on the best-seller list and climbing
was something called How To Cheat on Your Husband and Stay Happily Married. *There had been no*
movie offers yet.

Number two on the best-seller list was written by

a fifteen-year-old girl. It was called The Love Slave *and it swept the country like an electric broom. It had a six-figure paperback sale and the movie rights were going for the same price.*

Ms. FEIFFER was raised in Italy, spent her adolescence in Los Angeles and in the fifties returned to Europe, where she became a free-lance photographer. She now lives in New York with her daughter Kate. She is a production executive with Warner Bros. *A Hot Property* is her first novel.